*A
Harlequin
Romance*

1428

NIGHT OF THE SINGING BIRDS

by

SUSAN BARRIE

HARLEQUIN BOOKS

WINNIPEG ● CANADA

First published in 1970 by Mills & Boon Limited,
50 Grafton Way, Fitzroy Square, London, England.

SBN 373-01428-7

© Mills & Boon 1970

Harlequin Canadian edition published September, 1970
Harlequin U.S. edition published December, 1970

Printed in Canada

CHAPTER I

THERE were three women kneeling on the floor at her feet, and on the faces of two of them Angela watched expressions of fanatical zeal and devotion to the task in hand crowding all other expressions out of their tense and concentrated and somewhat elderly features. The other was a much younger woman, a novice at this sort of thing—a recent addition, in fact, to the establishment of *Madame Renée*, of Paris—and her principal function in life appeared at the moment to be the collecting of pins and holding of measuring tapes when they were thrust at her by one or other of the other two women.

Angela could feel the heat of the room sapping her energy and blunting the edges of her wits. It actually seemed to be coming at her in waves, and in them the sharp outlines of the furniture and the suffocating thickness of the carpet seemed to dissolve and be about to disappear as if they were no more than a mirage.

She pushed the heavy burnt-gold hair back from her brow, and protested that she must surely have been standing for far longer than was reasonable. Certainly in such a climate, and with the noise of the cicadas outside the windows creating a clamour that was enough in itself to give one a headache.

Madame Renée, who had made this journey specially from Paris to give satisfaction to one of her oldest and most valued clients, looked up in a vague way and sought to remember that the girl was young, and therefore some allowance had to be made for her and her inability to rise fully to such an occasion.

'If I could sit down for just a few minutes,' Angela requested a trifle faintly.

'*Mais certainement, mademoiselle,*' Madame Renée replied. 'But first I will remove the dress!' she added, with an expression of genuine horror lest some accident at this late stage should befall the confection in satin and lace that was one of her greatest causes for satisfaction at the moment.

The dress was removed, with such infinite care that it was some little while before Angela could utter a long-drawn sigh of relief and revel in the sensation of being free of the clinging satin and the hampering closeness of the waist and hiplines. Then she wandered over to the nearest window and extended her arms to the slight puff of air that came in at it.

Madame Renée regarded her a little thoughtfully. She was too immature to give her a feeling of *absolute* satisfaction in a job that would undoubtedly be well done. A little more flesh on the bones, in the right places, fewer hollows in the neck, and definitely a better developed bust would have provided her with more of a challenge, and drawn murmurs of awe from the beholders once the wedding gown was an established fact. At the moment the hemline was wavering, and in order to emphasise that slim waistline something would have to be done about the thirty-two-inch bust.

Padding, perhaps? ... She doubted whether Doña Miranda would consent to that. Members of the Cazenta d'Ialgo family were unlikely to make concessions, and although Angela was only half a Cazenta d'Ialgo—an uncompromising English Grevil, in fact, who most unfortunately took entirely after her father's family—the limitations would be the same, particularly as Doña Miranda, her grandmother, was footing the bill for the entire bridal outfit.

Madame Renée tapped her teeth with the end of the gold-mounted pencil with which she made calculations in connection with her client on a slip of paper that frequently got lost, with the result that the calculations had to be made all over again, and reflected that she would have to talk earnestly to Doña Miranda and persuade her that in this case *something would have to be done*.

Not that the girl was unattractive. Straight from her finishing school in Switzerland, she was all, and rather more, than one might have expected. She had escaped the Cazenta pallor, for one thing, and had an enchanting magnolia pale skin with a delicious hint of colour just over the cheekbones—when she wasn't being fitted for her wedding gown, and the temperature was very high, that is. And her hair was lovely and her eyes quite remarkable —like blue lakes in summertime. She had fluttering eyelashes, too, that were brown-gold at the tips, and a shapely little chin that was unexpectedly firm. And her mouth ... Well, in a year or two it would draw men's eyes as surely as if it was a magnet, Madame Renée felt convinced. And because she was a romantic at heart she hoped that it would.... Not, perhaps, the eyes of Don Felipe Martinez, who was to be her bridegroom, and was not merely a good many years older than his future bride but definitely rather hard-bitten and experienced in the ways of the world. But someone ... some time! ...

And then Madame Renée had the grace to feel somewhat ashamed of herself, and a little uncomfortable. For this was a Spanish bride she was dressing, and a very conventional Spanish bride.

There could be no question of affairs for her.

'Would you like some coffee, or perhaps a very small cognac?' she suggested, preparing to ring the bell. 'It is true that you have been standing for rather a long while.'

But Angela, revelling in the comparative coolness by the window, shook her head.

'No, thanks. I'll be all right in a minute.... But I find all these preparations a bit exhausting.' Her delicate brows puckered as she caught sight of the gleaming bonnet of a car that was turning in at the entrance to the courtyard below the window. The car was slightly rakish, long and low, of the same thick cream colour as Devonshire cream, and with attractively contrasting sky-blue upholstery. It also appeared to have many glittering attachments as it came to rest before the main entrance door of the villa.

Angela's brows, that were considerably darker than her hair, positively contracted as she recognised both the car and its occupant.

'It is Don Felipe,' she said, and backed automatically from the window.

Madame Renée and her two assistants just as automatically gravitated towards the window. She was so interested and intrigued that she forgot to warn her client that she was clad only in a pale peach-coloured slip, and that the balcony outside the window did not render it impossible for anyone glancing upwards rather suddenly to see her.

But Don Felipe was not the type who glanced upwards with much curiosity, even when the house contained the woman he was planning to marry. A Romeo of the true type might have been all eyes and ears and expectations, but Don Felipe had come from a consultation with his solicitors who were drawing up various documents in connection with the marriage settlements, and other details in connection with the marriage itself. He felt that he had provided very handsomely for the woman who was to become Señora Martinez, and share the elevation of his position in life; and even her maternal grandmother, Doña Miranda Cazenta d'Ialgo, would find little to complain of when the documents were submitted to her for her approval.

Another important piece of business he had transacted that morning was concerned with a visit to his bank, where a strong-box had been brought up from the vaults and the Martinez jewels displayed in broad daylight for the first time for quite a number of years. Felipe had opened case after case and decided that the contents would have to be sent away to be cleaned and re-set in a slightly more modern setting. He did not approve of anything ultra-modern, but a girl of nineteen had to have some sort of consideration meted out to her. And there was no doubt about it, many of the rings and brooches and heavy necklaces could not be worn as they were.

He would sacrifice his feeling for continuity and make a few concessions.

He was actually feeling rather pleased with himself as he alighted from his car, and without glancing upwards for a moment strode towards the entrance to the villa. The young woman he was to marry could think herself fortunate, since so much was being done to secure her happiness and well-being in the future. Certainly her grandmother would share his opinion, and as he admired and respected Doña Miranda that pleased him.

The sunshine was falling like golden rain from a brilliantly blue sky that was utterly without sign of cloud as he ran lightly up the steps. The courtyard was heavy with scent and hot with dust from the brazen hillsides as he turned into a cool colonnade, crossed another courtyard where a fountain played refreshingly in a marble basin, and was out of sight of the upstairs windows; and then, as the main door was standing open, entered the marble-floored hall of the villa.

Madame Renée and her assistants sighed regretfully. They had been permitted a glimpse of an extremely attractive masculine figure, dark and sleek as his Spanish ancestry demanded, taller than most Spaniards, and with well-held shoulders—he was a first-class tennis-player, and most of his winters were spent skiing down mountain sides. And as for riding and sailing ... well, he had yet to mount a horse that could succeed in unseating him, and he had his own yacht and was interested in water-polo.

The white-hot sunlight of Granada did wonderful things for his satin-smooth black hair, and like Angela he had quite a noticeable jaw ... softened in her case because she was feminine. And Madame Renée, who had been presented to him quite recently, knew that he had a pair of lustrous, if slightly mocking, dark eyes.

She was not a woman to be made to feel uncomfortable, even when circumstances were against her, but Don Felipe Martinez had actually, for some reason, made her feel just a little uncomfortable and by no means as sure as she usually was of the eminence she thought she had created for herself in life.

What sort of an effect he would have on a girl like Angela she actually shuddered to think ... unless, of course, she was in love with him. And if Angela Grevil, who was being groomed for marriage, was in love, then Madame was slipping. She was actually being deceived.

CHAPTER II

ANGELA, who had been pulling a dress over her head, and doing it rather awkwardly and hastily while her fiancé was making his way into the presence of her grandmother, emerged with her hair a little ruffled and a complete absence of anything that could be described as either joy or excitement in her face to meet the sudden smirk on the lips of Madame Renée, and the obvious insinuation in her eyes despite her own very private beliefs.

'The session is ended, *mademoiselle*,' she told her, as if she understood perfectly that it would be downright cruelty to detain her when anyone so vitally important to her whole future happiness had arrived. 'Señor Martinez is here, and of course he will wish to see you! ... *You* cannot wait to see him! We will deal with the matter of the hem another day. For the moment there is enough to attend to with the embroidery on the bodice and the going-away clothes——'

But Angela ran a hasty comb through her hair and shook her head.

'It is all right, *madame* ... Don Felipe is not here to see me! He will have come for a word with my grandmother.'

'But, *mademoiselle*! ...' arching her eyebrows dramatically.

Angela replaced the gold-mounted comb on the dressing-table, that was littered with all sorts of toilet bottles, and was the most delightfully feminine thing in the room, and took a long, probing look at herself in the mirror.

'You are French, *madame*,' she reminded her. 'Are not these things sometimes arranged in France?'

'Ah, *oui*!' Madame pretended to look enlightened. And then her whole face puckered as she strove to express denial of such a situation, and thrust out her hands. 'But you are so young, *mademoiselle*!' she protested. 'So young, and—if one is permitted to say so!—so pretty!' Secretly she thought she would be prettier in a year or so's time. 'And when your wedding dress is finished you will look quite *ravissante*.... And also, you are partly English,' she added, as if that altered the situation whichever way you looked at it, the English being a different breed from either the French or the Spanish.

The girl smiled bleakly at her reflection in the mirror and admitted as much.

'My father was English,' she agreed.

'And you bear an English name. The English are terribly independent!' Once again she thrust out her hands, as if she had encountered that independence on more than one occasion to her cost.

Angela continued to smile, without any actual

14

brightening of her eyes, and wielded a lipstick experimentally.

'This is too pale for me,' she declared, as she viewed the result with distaste. 'It is much too young-girlish. I should like to be more sophisticated!'

But Madame Renée shook her head at her, and for the first time offered her a piece of advice which she knew was quite valuable.

'No, no, *mademoiselle*, you must not grow up too soon! It is a great mistake! When once the ageing process begins it travels at speed, and that is a thing all women must deplore!' With a nod of her head she indicated to the other two that they could commence gathering up the wedding gown and all the attendant materials, and then she walked across to the dressing-table and laid a hand —rather hard and bony-looking, but marvellously deft when handling costly silks—on her youthful customer's arm.

'Listen, my dear,' she said, speaking in English, 'you will find that your double nationality will harm you a little at times. The English are not merely independent, they carry this independence to extremes ... and if only you were one hundred per cent Spanish, or even one hundred per cent French, you would look forward to your marriage with delight. It would not matter to you in the least that Don Felipe is so much older, and so very much more experienced. But as it is——!' And she rolled her eyes expressively.

'As it is?' Angela looked at her intently, with sudden interest. 'As it is, *madame*...?'

The older woman laid a cautious finger to her lips, and looked warningly at the two other occupants of the room.

'I should not speak to you like this, Miss Grevil, and your esteemed grandmother might find it hard to thank me if I offer you some advice.... But I feel that I must, all the same! You see, I have English blood myself—in fact, my mother was English!—and I know what it is to feel—well, outside things! These arranged marriages—so practical, so very sensible from so very many points of view, and so extremely unromantic—do sometimes turn out to be the most sensible marriages of all! They can even be happy marriages, but it is a matter of bringing the right approach to them ... the right——'

She sought for a word, which her limited amount of contact with her mother's family made difficult, and Angela helped her out.

'The right attitude of mind?' The sea-blue English eyes sparkled contemptuously. 'A submissive attitude?'

Madame Renée nodded her head.

'It is always better to submit,' she said. 'To fight does nothing but harm oneself!'

Angela tried to look appreciative of the other woman's good intentions, but the antagonistic sparkle remained in her eyes.

'I will see what I can do about it, *madame*,' she

16

promised.

There came a light tap on the door, and a smartly uniformed sleek-haired maid put in her head. With the same amount of awe in her voice that might have been expected to be there if she had been about to announce a miracle, she declared:

'The Señor Don Felipe Martinez is waiting to see you, *señorita*! He is in the *salón*! ...He says that he has little time to spare, so will you be so good as to hurry and not keep him waiting!'

Angela and Madame Renée looked at one another. Madame Renée smiled and nodded encouragingly.

'Remember that you will look *très charmante* on the day!' she urged. 'I, personally, will see to that!'

Angela did not actually thank her, but she sent her a thoughtful look and then hurried after the maid along the corridor. The house, at that hour, was as still as a pool—barely an hour before the silver-toned gong in the hall announced luncheon —and the polished marble flags in the hall reflected the outlines of the handsome black oak Spanish furniture as if they were indeed composed of water, with an iridescent shimmer where a determined shaft of the bright sunlight outside found its way through one of the slats of the securely closed green shutters. The dimness rendered the place mysterious, and it certainly helped the coolness, which was additionally aided by whirring electric fans, although there was nothing in the way of air-conditioning.

Doña Miranda, unlike many Spanish women of her class, liked to be surrounded by flowers, and they gleamed waxily in the gloom as Angela and the maid walked past towering erections of blooms that were heavily scented, and mingled with the perfume of a cigarette that the man who had been waiting impatiently in the *salón*, and had just stepped out into the hall to meet them, had absent-mindedly crushed out in a fine specimen of a pot-plant that was sharing a *jardinière* with other plants.

He realised too late what he had done, and muttered irritably to himself. Why did women have to surround themselves with these things? His own mother amongst them! Flowers were meant to grow in a garden, and not to be brought into a house.

'Ah, *buenos días, señorita*!' He bowed low before his fiancée, and then possessed himself of her hand and kissed it lightly. 'I trust that I have not burst in upon you at an inconvenient moment? Doña Miranda said something about you being shut away from the world with your dressmaker. . . . But even dressmakers have to be dismissed when other, more pressing, problems have to be dealt with. And it is a question of a setting for a sapphire ring!'

'Oh yes?' But there was little enthusiasm in Angela's tone as she glanced at him for a moment. She led the way into the *salón*, which he had just vacated. 'I have been receiving fittings for my wedding gown, *señor*, but no doubt to a man that is scarcely important.'

There was great dryness in her tone, and to say that it astonished him was no understatement. He glanced at her far more sharply and alertly than she had glanced at him, observed that she was wearing something pale and cool in linen, and that her burnt-gold hair was quite casually caught back with a hair-ribbon that took at least four years off her acknowledged nineteen, and was the same colour as her dress, and thought—as he had thought once or twice before—that in some ways she was rather a curious and an aloof little thing.

But that, no doubt, was because she was partly English. He had spent a few years of his life in England himself, receiving his education at a famous public school, and he had seen girls like her on Speech Days, and at strawberry teas on the lawns of English country houses. No one would have guessed, had they not already been aware of the fact, that she was Spanish both by birth and upbringing, despite the fact that her father was an Englishman.

Born here in this very villa, where the sun scorched every blade of grass and rendered the hillsides sere and yellow for at least three-fifths of the year. The remaining two-fifths provided sufficient nutriment for crops to mature and the simplest cottage garden to be a blaze of flowers when tourists came seeking the sun and prepared to soak up the colour of the sunsets and dawns as if they were eager sponges that could never have enough.

But a naturally cool temperament like an English temperament was bound to be resistant to a certain extent, and Doña Miranda's granddaughter would never be completely Spanish. Doña Miranda might have done her best to eradicate certain English failings, and to anticipate certain possible eventualities despite the effect of environment, but her guardianship even from her own point of view had not been an entire success. She had had charge of Angela from the moment of her birth, for her daughter had been too frail to survive it on top of the bitter disappointment of her alien husband's death as the result of a riding accident, and it had been left to the old and experienced woman to supervise an upbringing that had been by no means strictly conventional from the point of view of a highly conventional Spaniard.

True, Angela had had instilled in her all the right kind of ideas and beliefs about conventional behaviour and social conduct. But she had also been sent away to school, in direct defiance of the established tradition of Cazenta d'Ialgo women; and in addition to that schooling she had had a finishing course at an up-to-date finishing school in Switzerland. She had absorbed ideas and attitudes, become infected with notions that were hardly Spanish, or so Don Felipe decided when he was first presented to her at a meeting arranged by her grandmother. It could not honestly be said that he fell in love with her, but she was charming and personable—rather more than personable—and despite a certain air of aggressiveness, reasonably submissive.

It could not honestly be said that she was as submissive as her cousin Jacinta, whom he had at one time contemplated marrying, but if she had acquired convictions she had not yet acquired the courage to stand up for them. She was basically shy and diffident, and it boded well for a reasonably satisfactory marriage, if that shyness and diffidence were encouraged rather than discouraged.

Besides, there was something about her looks that appealed to him. It could have been the bright, unusual hair and the sea-blue eyes and fluttering eyelashes, the mutinous little chin and the unpredictable mouth. And, far more important than all that, she was the possessor of estates that marched well with his, and it had become a burning ambition of his to unite those estates.

Doña Miranda agreed with him, and so did all the uncles and aunts on the Ialgo side. A marriage that was to take place almost immediately seemed an excellent notion, and now it was just a matter of getting all the details settled and various signatures on documents and things like that.

But of course the girl herself had to be given some reason for looking forward to the marriage, and presumably a lot of new clothes was one reason that appealed to her. He smiled at her in rather a calculating and extraordinarily charming way, despite the calculation, and handed her the ring case for her consideration.

'That is one of the most flawless sapphires you are ever likely to see in the whole of your lifetime,' he told her, as he watched her snap open the case and gaze at the slightly cumbersome trinket it contained.

Angela slipped the ring from its satin bed and on to her finger. It felt heavy and unwanted, and because she had no great interest in sapphires she took it off hurriedly.

'It is indeed a very fine stone, *señor*,' she agreed flatly.

He smiled, and his excellent white teeth created a dazzling blur in his dark and even-featured face. One eyebrow went upwards a little whimsically.

'And that is all you can find to say about it? You are not impressed?—Not really?'

'On the contrary,' she assured him stiffly, 'I am very much impressed, *señor*.'

He continued to smile, but somewhat wryly. He took her hand and slid the ring up and down her slender white finger—the finger that was soon to be further burdened by his wedding ring—and exclaimed because it was such a very slender finger, with a rosy nail that was highly polished, and the ring was far, far and away too large for her.

'You must supply me with one of your gloves, *cara*,' he said, 'and that will ensure that the new fitting will be exactly right. As to the setting, you can leave that, I think, to me.'

'Yes, *señor*,' she agreed.

A vaguely vexed expression crossed his face.

'I find your formality a little surprising,' he confessed, 'in a young woman so soon to be married. Did you not tell me that you have been receiving fittings for your wedding gown?'

'Yes, *señor*.'

'Then would it not be more natural if you addressed me as Felipe, and not *señor*? If we are to go through a married life in such a formal state of mind it will be very trying.'

'Very well, *señor* ... I mean Felipe!'

His dark eyes gazed at her as if he thought it might be as well to humour her, and then he turned away and walked to the window, the ring case safely restored to his pocket.

Angela had hurried to the window the moment they entered the room and flung open one of the shutters, and he could see the blinding light in the courtyard falling in a dazzling fashion across the black and white tiled floor, and the boxes and tubs of colourful growth being scorched by it.

'I noticed,' he observed, gazing upwards at the hard blue of the sky, that was without even a tiny white cloud scudding across it, 'that you did not find the dimness of this room restful. You have the English habit of throwing open windows.'

She looked somewhat taken aback, because he sounded distinctly critical.

'I—I suppose I got used to doing that in England,' she admitted. 'And Switzerland,' she added.

'Both basically cool places.' He turned and

looked at her. 'You were at school in England?'

'Yes.'

'You liked it? You felt, perhaps, that you belonged there?'

'I—I wouldn't say that.' And then she decided to be strictly youthful—she had enjoyed every minute of her schooldays in England, and she had found Spain suffocating in more ways than one when she returned to it. The thought of cool English grass, soft breezes coming in at the window, the smell of clove pinks and roses floating in the warmth of a summer dusk, made her feel like someone who was being deprived. She moistened her lips with the tip of her tongue, and her throat worked. He could see the slender, shapely little white throat emerging from the pale linen of her dress, and the thought occurred to him that he might even span it with one of his lean, brown hands.

Sharply he asked her:

'You have returned to Spain, but you are not happy here? Is that it?'

Once more she licked her lips.

'I—I expect I will grow used to it.'

'But it is your country.... You will have to live here for the rest of your life! Does that thought not fill you with some sort of satisfaction?'

'Not—not much, *señor*.'

Impatiently he turned aside. She knew that his fingers were clutching the ring case in his pocket, and that they were hard, impatient fingers, just as his temper was of the fiery order that very quickly got out of hand. Meeting the frustrated, rather bewildered gleam in his exceptionally lustrous and really rather beautiful dark eyes—extraordinary that a man should have beautiful eyes, she thought —and sensing that he wasn't merely baffled by her attitude but inclined to look upon her as rather a ridiculous young woman who might be improved by a good slap where it might hurt her most, she actually felt herself recoil from him.

She hadn't had much time to think about it before, but now it suddenly struck her that he was rather a terrifying member of his sex, and the fact that he was a hundred per cent Spanish made him more terrifying still. As an acquaintance—someone to sit beside her at a dinner-party, or even partner her at a dance—he might be acceptable; but as a man it had been arranged she should marry, who would have the right to order her life for her once she was married to him, and might find her just as difficult to get along with, he was—nothing short of terrifying.

The thought that she was going to marry him suddenly filled her with cold horror. He could see it mounting in her eyes as they gazed at him, feel it quivering in the contracting muscles of her throat and the sudden tight clenching of her hands held rigidly at her sides.

Even he suddenly asked himself if he wasn't doing something quite ridiculous, marrying this girl.... And then he recollected all the advantages of such a union, and he told himself the whole situation was just simply absurd, and all he had to do to improve matters was to get to know the girl.

Of course! Why had it never occurred to him before that she was not quite as other Spanish girls were? In fact, very far removed from being a Spanish girl! She looked English, and to all intents and purposes, apparently, she was English, and something would have to be done about it.

'I have your grandmother's consent to take you out to dinner to-night,' he told her. 'There is a *fiesta* in the town. Would you care to entrust yourself to me and see something of it?'

'I—I——'

She was quite appalled by the prospect.

He looked rather more than impatient—in fact, she was inclined to suspect that he would boil over at any moment.

'*Well?*'

'I—er—Y-yes, thank you, *señor*—Felipe! I would enjoy it very much indeed,' she told him as if he had demanded from her an acknowledgement that she would enjoy having all her teeth extracted. 'It is—please believe me that I think it is!—very good of you to suggest it!'

He turned away. And then he turned back to her and bowed stiffly.

'I will call for you at eight o'clock this evening. Please do not keep me waiting when I arrive!' he requested formally.

CHAPTER III

IT was already dark when he called for her. The night closes down swiftly in that southern province, and it seemed to Angela a pity that so much of the magnificent splendour of Andalusia was lost to her when they set off in his powerful cream car.

But before that she had to spend half an hour waiting for him to collect her, and during that half-hour she sat and talked to her grandmother in her grandmother's ornate bedchamber.

The old lady retired to bed early these days, and already she was ready for her maid to settle her down amongst the pillows of her great bed, made of Spanish mahogany, and with an overhanging tester that was more like a catafalque. Robed in a voluminous dressing gown and with her splendid dark hair—not one sign of grey lurked amongst the sable darkness—smoothed and braided for the night, she sipped a cup of hot chocolate and discussed with her only granddaughter the possibilities of the evening ahead of her.

Angela was dressed in white—an enchanting shift-like dress in wild silk—and with it she wore the usual hair-ribbon looped through her hair. Only to-night it was worn like an Alice band, and the hair was flowing loose on her shoulders. Doña Miranda was secretly very proud of that hair, just as she had been secretly very proud of the son-in-law who had been a member of the family for such a very short while before his fatal accident.

To a Spanish woman, accustomed to the swarthiness of her countrymen, the exceptional fairness of Brian Grevil had been nothing short of miraculous. Even for an Anglo-Saxon he was an outstanding example of how utterly arresting a fair-haired, fair-skinned man with blue eyes can appear when viewed against a background of alien Latin types. His hair had been much fairer than his daughter's, and his eyes a lighter, sunnier blue. But she had inherited the excellent quality of his features, as well as the slenderness of his build. At the moment the one thing that worried Doña Miranda about her—apart from her marked English temperament —was her lack of curves of the right kind. By that the Spanish woman, if asked, would have explained that she meant seductive curves.

For according to her view a woman who lacked seductiveness was unlikely to earn the full appreciation of her husband. And although, unfortunately for a large number of Spanish women, they did very quickly outgrow their seductiveness and become positively fat and forbidding, it was better to be plump at the right time than never to be plump at all.

The fact that Doña Miranda herself was extremely thin, and rather raw-boned, no doubt inclined her somewhat strongly to this view.

'You will enjoy yourself, child,' she said, 'if you forget to be afraid of Don Felipe. He is to be your husband, and the sooner you overcome your awe of him the better. It is natural, of course, that you should regard him with some awe—as well as, of course, admiration. But to look at him as if he petrifies you as soon as he makes an appearance in the same room as yourself is another matter altogether.'

Angela looked faintly guilty, but there was one thing she had to get clear.

'I am not at all sure that I do admire him, *Abuela*,' she confessed. 'In fact, I do not think I admire him at all. He is far too alarming to be admired.'

Doña Miranda looked impatient.

'Nonsense, child. There is nothing in the least alarming about Felipe. I knew his mother and his grandmother, and he has always treated me with affection. I am really quite fond of him already, although he has yet to become my grandson-in-law. It is true that with you it is slightly different—you have been at school too long, and you have seen hardly anything at all of the men of your race. They are handsome and virile, and should be the answer to every young girl's dream. So if you formed some attachment for some visiting tutor in Switzerland you must forget him. In any case, the Swiss make appalling husbands!'

'I have formed no attachment for any man I

have yet met, *Abuela*,' her granddaughter told her gravely, as if she suspected that at her age that was a trifle odd. 'As a matter of fact——'

'Yes?'

'Although some of the girls at Madame Dupont's *did* develop crushes when they went on holiday, and for the school doctor, I have always been a little bored by the society of men.' Her tone was so prim and restrained that Doña Miranda smiled to herself, thinking this was a very un-Spanish tendency. 'There are so many things in life that I want to do, and being married to a man is not one of them. I don't even want to be mistress of my own house, and I'd rather look after other people's children than have some of my own. In fact——'

'*Yes?*' more sharply than before.

'It did occur to me at one time that I—well, that I might take up nursing, or something that would involve me with children—That was before you decided that I must marry Don Felipe!'

'Rubbish! The only children you will concern yourself with will be your own.'

'But I would far rather——'

Doña Miranda held up a white, bony hand in a very disapproving manner.

'This is not the kind of talk I enjoy,' she stated stiffly. 'In fact, I am quite horrified by it. An engaged girl——'

'But, Grandmother——!' Angela got up from her chair and moved eagerly nearer to her—she even knelt on the floor at her feet. 'I am not yet twenty, and there really *are* a number of things I want to do that I will be quite unable to do once I am married.' The words poured forth eagerly, in a soft flood. 'I have a house in England that I have only visited on one occasion, and enough money to go and live there, and—and breed horses——'

'*Horses?*' in horrified accents.

'Yes; I—I ride well ... and I could teach horse-riding——'

'Over my dead body!' the older woman declared.

Angela sighed, and sat back on her ankles.

'Then I have friends, who have invited me to stay—one friend in particular. She, too, is interested in horses, and in fact she hunts ... and her brother hunts, too!'

'Her brother?' The older woman's eyes rolled. 'The sooner we get you married the better, my dear, and it might be as well if the marriage date is put forward. I will speak to Don Felipe to-night. And thank goodness your wedding gown is practically finished, and all the details of your trousseau. Had I had the least idea that you were thinking like this I would have been most alarmed....' She certainly looked alarmed, and her fine eyes flashed with annoyance and bewilderment. 'To think that a Cazenta d'Ialgo should have such disloyal thoughts and aspirations when she is formally betrothed, and should be thinking instead how very, very fortunate she is to have contracted such an alliance.'

'You mean, *you* contracted the alliance for me, *Abuela*,' Angela pointed out with very English dryness. 'And I am not really a Cazenta d'Ialgo,' she added. 'I am a Grevil. I like to think of myself as a Grevil.'

'Why, certainly, since your father was a Grevil. But that does not mean that you are not also one of us. I hope you will never forget that your mother's family is one of the finest in Spain. You should be immensely proud of the Spanish blood in your veins.'

Angela gave up. She was by no means clear why she had suddenly, as it were, gone off the rails like this ... and of course she was proud of being a Cazenta d'Ialgo. But certainly not as proud as her grandmother was. And despite the fact that a Spanish landscape, a Spanish sunset—and, in particular, Spanish moonlight—affected her in a way that nothing else had ever yet quite done, she was sure that every drop of blood in her veins was pure English. She neither thought nor reacted as a Spanish woman did, and as a matter of fact she despised the attitude of mind of Spanish women that permitted them to accept a second-class role in Life.

Once she was married—once she was Doña Martinez—she, too, would step back into a pattern that had been repeated for generations, and would probably go on being repeated for as many generations in the future unless the backwash of a changing world affected Spain as it seemed most unlikely it would do at the present time.

Her face must have reflected a certain resignation which temporarily deprived it of much of the lustre of its youth, for quite unexpectedly Doña Miranda softened, and she bent forward and touched Angela's smooth, pale cheek with an unusually caressing bony forefinger.

'Ah, child,' she said, 'you are talking a lot of nonsense, but that is because you are young, and even I when I was young did not always conform in the way that was expected of me. I can remember quite clearly that I had moments of rebellion.... We all have moments of rebellion! But Don Felipe Martinez is everything I could desire for you in a husband, and when you go out with him to-night you must think only that he *is* the right man for you, who will safeguard your future and care for your well-being as every good husband should, and once your children come along you will not feel the need to care for other people's! Believe me, I know!' And all at once she smiled, and there was just a hint of secrecy and mystery in that smile.

Angela smiled back, with the same amount of secrecy and reservation.

'And it is not necessary to love a man before you marry him?'

'Certainly not! Love does not enter into it.'

'Not even once you are married?'

'Sometimes—sometimes one grows to love the man one marries.'

'But in your opinion affection and obedience are

enough?'

Doña Miranda smiled a trifle more astringently. 'You must not quote me, child—not in matters of this sort. But as a general principle you can take it that a woman's most prominent rôle in life is to care for and plan for her children, and the greater part of the love in her life should be lavished upon them.'

'Just as you lavished it upon my mother?'

'I—I suppose so.'

The old eyes and the young ones met. Years ago Doña Miranda had been a remarkably handsome woman, with much fire in her eyes and veins. Even to-day the fire was capable of being rekindled, but at the moment she looked a trifle wry.

'Yes,' she said, more decidedly. 'A woman's place is in the background of a man's life. I personally believe that.'

'Liar!' Angela thought to herself, with a feeling of warmth and softness towards her grandmother welling up like a spring in her heart. Then a maid came to inform her that Don Felipe had arrived to collect her, and she turned without another word and followed the girl from the room.

Don Felipe was looking almost unbelievably handsome and quite spectacularly well-groomed in a white dinner-jacket and cummerbund, and that his mood was urbane it was easy for Angela to gather from the almost paternal way in which he smiled at her and greeted her.

He took her hand and turned it delicately about

and kissed the inside of her wrist, where she had not omitted to add a touch of perfume before she left her room. And then he complimented her on her appearance, not as if he was in any way affected by it himself, but as if he was mildly surprised she had taken quite so many pains to appear at her best in his company. It occurred to Angela that he was half expecting her to look a trifle sulky, and he had possibly expected her to have selected one of her least attractive gowns for the occasion, such as the black which did not become her but which so many Spanish women wore as a kind of uniform. But the girl's enchanting white dress, with its exquisite embroidery, lent her a rare look—even if at the same time it emphasised her youth, which as a man who was committed to marry her he could have disapproved of. A girl of marriageable age should look as if she was ready for matrimony, with all its attendant cares—if Doña Miranda was to be believed. And Angela Grevil still had something of the schoolroom and the cloistered life clinging about her. She had been taught to behave so beautifully that she almost did it too well. And in addition she looked so uncompromisingly English.

For just one instant a rather wry look invaded his eyes before he released her hand. And then he said crisply:

'Well then, we will go, shall we? You are, I trust, looking forward to the evening ahead of us?'

She assured him that she was, and he actually flashed her a white-toothed, dubious smile.

'In that case I must see that you are not disappointed,' he said.

They set off in his car, and not for the first time in his company she wished he was not quite so addicted to slightly reckless speed. Not that she imagined for one moment that he was capable of losing control of a car. His strong and shapely hands on the wheel, and his whole attitude of assurance, prevented her having any doubts on that score.

But she was not fond of speed for speed's sake. And at that hour of the evening there was a soft, sensuous warmth in the atmosphere, after the more brazen heat of the day, that was stirred up by their swift passage through the starlit night.

As yet there was no moon, but the stars were very bright. Angela loved the fertility of the wide valley wherein the Moors had set down Granada, and all that triumphant colour that was Andalusia, and she wished they had set off a little earlier, while there was still light enough left by the sunset to show her the richness and abundance of the flowers, fruit and grain that she knew were extending on all sides of her; while the Sierra Nevada, rising in a solid bulk against the sky, would have brought the excited breath catching in her throat while they were still highlighted by the fires of sunset.

As it was, everything was seen through a richly purple haze, and on it the perfume of the tobacco plantations floated in sensuous clouds. It stirred her blood, despite the fact that it was so balanced and English ... and as the moon climbed slowly into the sky, and everything surrounding her was drenched in a miraculous flood of silver, she wondered why it was that her thoughts harked back so constantly to England, and why she actually craved to spend some part of her life there.

She loved Spain. She knew that she loved it quite passionately at times. But never could she quite overcome the feeling that it was alien country, and that her roots lay in a cooler clime altogether. She had dreamed that if she ever married and settled down it would be in England. But now, all at once, she actually failed to understand her constant preoccupation with a land that had not even figured prominently in her upbringing, although it was true she owned a house there. Why could she not settle down and live happily in Spain? Or, at any rate, why could she not make up her mind to make the *effort* to concentrate on living happily in Spain, with a man whom lots of young women of her age—including a number of her old schoolfellows —would have been thrilled to bits by the very idea of living with him and his vast estates and splendid income in a land that was all colour and warmth and enchantment by comparison with duller and more northerly climes?

She glanced at him, but he was concentrating fixedly on driving, and it struck her, not for the first time by any means, that unless he was making a deliberate effort to entertain her he seemed to have very little desire to talk to her. There was usually a little frown between his well-marked black brows when he was concentrating on something quite apart from her, and it was there now ... as if his thoughts worried him, and the soothing perfume of the tobacco plants had failed to have any effect on him.

They entered the town to find that it was taken over by tourists, and the steep and narrow streets were thronged with them. Granada has so much to offer the tourist that it was small wonder they were milling around in lightly clothed bevies, while the hotels were doing most satisfactory big business. From the courts of the Alhambra, where tall cypresses swayed dreamily against the sky, to the small Arab-style shops in the Zacatin, a feeling of holiday—of *fiesta*—was affecting the spirits of everyone. The more affluent sipped cocktails on hotel terraces, the young and the adventurous and the more homely roved the streets and waited for the fireworks that would provide such a spectacular show later on.

Angela had no real idea where her escort was taking her to dine, but she strongly suspected it would be somewhere extremely respectable. She was perfectly right, for despite the crush they were received by deferential waiters in a somewhat unusual hotel that was more like a centuries-old inn, with a Moorish-style décor and an extremely exclusive clientele. They sipped aperitifs on the terrace while their table was made ready for them, and afterwards Angela found herself ensconced with her husband-to-be in a discreet corner of a flower-filled room, and pressed to decide upon what she would like to eat. She decided to leave all matter of choice to Don Felipe, and he proved his experience by selecting for her the very things she would herself have chosen if she had not considered it more diplomatic in a woman to leave the ordering to him.

The wine he ordered was not, as she had half expected it would be, champagne, but a light and very pleasant local wine that was quite unlikely to have any disastrous after-effects, and she doubted whether she could have become intoxicated on it even had she allowed herself more than one or two glasses. Don Felipe himself had something slightly stronger, and he concluded the meal with a liqueur which he did not permit her, any more than it would even have occurred to him to offer her a cigarette.

As it happened she did not smoke, but she was slightly amused. The way he treated her was exactly the way he would have treated a favourite niece, or even a young sister, he was taking out to dine. Sweet things had to be selected for her, and of course there was lots of fruit, and a very special ice cream with fruit in it and a delectable colourful whip on the top of it.

Afterwards they returned to the terrace, and coffee was brought to them. From somewhere inside the hotel music reached them, but it was not music to which they could dance, like the throbbing guitar music that was being played across the street in a more modern and with-it hotel crammed to capacity with holiday-makers. Angela sat back in her chair and looked up at the brilliance of the sky above Granada, and just for one moment she wondered what it would be like to be taken out for a really gay evening, with Flamenco and eager, swaying bodies, tapping of heels and fluttering fans, a glistening floor on which anyone and everyone could tap and sway, too, and perhaps a careless wander through the moonlit streets afterwards.

She sighed, her lips parting a little without her knowledge ... and she saw that Don Felipe was regarding her a trifle quizzically on the softly-lit terrace.

'All is not well, little one?' he asked. 'Or is it simply that you are bored?'

She denied being bored almost indignantly, for if she had appeared bored then she was guilty of a lapse of good manners that troubled her. But she need not have worried. Felipe was not offended. He was racking his brains for something to say to her, something that would get through to whatever type of mind it was that lay behind her well-bred-young-woman exterior.

And then a party of people passed below them in the street. A woman looked up at him, ceased laughing lightheartedly at something one of her companions had just said to her, and then made for the foot of the steps and extended both hands as she moved towards Angela's escort.

'Why, *Felipe*!' she exclaimed, and her voice was as English as Angela's own. But nothing about Angela was as glamorous and unusual as the radiant creature the Spaniard, galvanised into delighted movement, rose to greet.

CHAPTER IV

'I WAS half hoping I might bump into you, but never thought I would do so in quite this fashion,' she said, as her hands lay in Felipe's and the two of them gazed at one another as if the meeting was pure pleasure on both sides. 'I could of course have contacted you before my arrival in Spain, but it occurred to me you might be on the other side of the world, and in any case I'm accompanied by friends. We're moving on all the time.'

'I still think you should have contacted me,' Felipe told her, declining to let go of her hands. 'You and your friends could have come and stayed with me. You know—you must know!—that you are always welcome as a visitor!'

She made a slight but engaging face.

'As a *visitor*, Felipe? Are we as distant as all that these days?'

He smiled at her.

'You and I could never be distant, Carmelita. . . .' And then he turned to the little group of people who had followed her up the steps to the terrace, and were standing rather awkwardly waiting to be acknowledged. 'Introduce me, please! Any friend of yours is my friend!'

The necessary introductions were made, and

there was a good deal of bowing and hand-shaking. The radiant young woman's escort comprised a couple of Spaniards and three English friends, and there was only one other young woman amongst them. She, too, appeared to be English, and she gazed at Don Felipe as if it had always been a secret dream of hers to meet someone of his exalted rank amongst exciting-looking Latins, and now that the dream had come true she was a little over-awed. Particularly as he saluted her hand with his lips in a way that it had never been saluted before.

Then, and only then, did he remember Angela. His newly discovered and very beautiful friend had been staring at her in the mellow flood of light that illuminated the terrace, and she was looking faintly quizzical when the Don at last presented her.

'Miss Angela Grevil, my fiancée,' he said. And as Angela stood up: 'Mrs. Martin Ruddock. Mrs. Ruddock's husband was a very close friend of mine.'

'Was?' Angela said to herself, since the husband didn't appear to be amongst Mrs. Ruddock's *coterie* of supporters. She extended a diffident hand, and Mrs. Ruddock took it.

'I'm a widow,' she explained sweetly. 'I've been a widow for exactly two years.'

And then her's, and the Don's eyes, met.

'Granada is *en fête* to-night,' Angela murmured mechanically. 'I expect you're hoping to see the fireworks.'

'Fireworks?' Mrs. Ruddock shrugged her shoulders. 'Does one really bother one's head about fire-works nowadays, when there are so many more entertaining things to be seen and to do? The thing I love about a crowd like this is that it lets its hair down, and even Spanish courting couples make love in doorways, and if you feel like dancing uninhibitedly you can. In fact, there's no point in wandering about the streets if you're going to be-have in a very prim and proper fashion.' She glanced upwards provocatively at Don Felipe. 'But I'll confess I can't imagine you behaving in any-thing but a prim and proper fashion in the streets of Granda, Felipe—or London or Paris, if it comes to that! You never forget your dignity!'

'Perhaps my dignity is all I have,' he replied, a bright sparkle of amusement in his handsome black eyes. Then he put her into a chair, and a waiter brought other chairs to their table. 'This is an occa-sion, I think, that calls for champagne,' he added. 'Juan, what is your favourite vintage year? Let us have something very special for my friends!'

'Si, señor,' Juan responded, and departed to carry out the order.

Mrs. Ruddock lay back in her chair, and as she was now immediately beneath one of the lights Angela could see that she was rather more than quite spectacularly lovely. She had hair that was not unlike her own, except that it was even fairer, and she wore it swathed about her head in a silken coil. Her dress was of midnight blue chiffon, rather short, permitting one to dwell on excellent legs, and she must have stepped out of her hotel just after dinner, for there were diamonds in her ears and diamonds sparkling at her neck and wrists, and her escorts were all smartly and properly attired for the evening. But for the presence of the other young woman Angela would have thought of her as a prize bloom being protected and cherished by a favoured band of the faithful, but the other young woman was attractive, too, only she certainly hadn't a pair of eyes like Mrs. Ruddock.

As she tipped back her head to look up at her host Angela could see them very clearly, huge, and smoky grey, with long fringes of (possibly false) thick black eyelashes. She was skilfully, but not too heavily, made up apart from the eyelashes, and her mouth was particularly arresting. Certainly, no man could have gazed at her for long without becoming conscious of it.

And when she smiled, the smile was like a deliberate act of seduction.

Angela caught herself up, wondering why her thoughts were wandering along such lines. And then it occurred to her that it was not perhaps surprising. The arrival of this young woman on the scene had resulted in an order for champagne, which a dinner she and her fiancé had sat through together, without anything in the nature of outside diversion, had apparently not called for. It had not been in any sense a celebration dinner.

'You know, Felipe,' Mrs. Ruddock told him, 'you really surprised me just now when you introduced me to Miss Grevil. For some reason I've never thought of you as a marrying man.'

'No?' He was bending towards her, offering her a cigarette, and the gleam of amusement persisted between his own thick dark eyelashes.

'Which was rather silly of me, I suppose,' Mrs. Ruddock continued, accepting the cigarette and allowing him to light it for her. Her eyes dwelt on him almost with absorption. 'You Spaniards are very family-minded, aren't you? And I expect you thought it was high time you got married!'

'Rather more than high time,' Felipe agreed with her. 'If I had had any real sense of responsibility and all that is expected of me I would have done so long ago.'

'But at least you are placating family interests now?' The huge eyes communicated a sense of amusement, of slightly derisive humour. 'I am sure you are thinking hopefully of an heir, and all that sort of thing. With estates like yours an heir is most important.... When do you get married?'

'In another five or six weeks.'

'Then the date is not fixed?'

'Not yet. Angela is in the midst of collecting clothes for the event.'

'Ah, the bridal trousseau!' She glanced alertly at Angela. 'How exciting!' she drawled. 'How madly exciting! I can recollect what fun I had collecting masses and masses of things I actually never wore when my own turn arrived, and I married Martin. Only he and I were so madly in love that I don't

46

think we thought of anything else apart from each other. The orgy of buying and the preparations were just an extra delight thrown in.'

'And now you are a widow,' Angela reminded her, understanding perfectly that she was not expected to insist that she was madly in love with Don Felipe. Perhaps it was so obvious that she wasn't in love, she thought afterwards.

Mrs. Ruddock nodded.

'But it was marvellous while it lasted,' she declared briefly. Then she looked across at Don Felipe and smiled brilliantly. 'Your fiancée is very pretty,' she told him, 'but I was astonished to hear that she has an English name—and, as a matter of fact, she looks very English. I had imagined, if you ever did marry, it would be a Spanish woman.'

For the first time he looked and sounded a little withdrawn.

'Angela is half Spanish,' he replied, 'and the half that is Spanish is an excellent half. On the English side I have no faults to find, either,' with a contemplative look directed at Angela.

'Oh, but, my dear, I never meant that you could possibly have cause to find fault with what is obviously an excellent arrangement,' the widow purred, with sudden dulcet softness. Then she smiled for the first time very sweetly at Angela. 'You must invite me to your wedding, child. If I am not in Spain I will fly over for the great event.' Once more she glanced at Felipe. 'I wouldn't miss it for the world!'

'Of course, if you would like to receive an invitation, *madame*, I will see to it that you are sent one...' Angela began diffidently, but the other interrupted her.

'For goodness' sake, my dear, don't be so formal,' she protested. 'The name is Willow, and you must call me that. Carmelita is Felipe's pet name for me, but I'll confess I've never thought of myself as a Carmelita. I'm much too fair and English, like yourself.... And I'm truly astonished that you've got any Spanish blood in your veins! Your children will be an exciting mixture. I wonder what they'll be like?'

Felipe once more bent towards her, and the very way in which he did so was the next best thing to an actual caress.

'Tell me, Carmelita,' he enquired of her softly, 'where are you staying? And for how long do you propose to honour Granada? We can't have you running home too soon——'

'Not home, Felipe, but on to the next port of call.' Her exciting mouth curved upwards, enticingly, at the corners. 'You forget that I am my own mistress, and nowadays I have few ties. I ran in to these good friends'—she waved a hand to indicate them—'in Seville, and we decided to have fun together. But now I am likely to be at a loose end again, for they are returning home in about another couple of days—all except José and Pedro here, of course,' smiling at the two Spaniards who had attached themselves to her retinue. 'You forget

48

that we English are hampered by a travel allowance, and it is most inconvenient at times,' and the lovely mouth set more petulantly.

But Don Felipe seemed to be inspired by a sudden notion.

'Then we must do all that we can to overcome this difficulty for you,' he said, with an eagerness that Angela for one had never associated with him. 'We must relieve you of the necessity of settling hotel bills! I cannot have you disappearing out of my life again so soon after you have consented to reappear in it, and perhaps your friends'—obviously, however, not including the two Spaniards, whom by his look he quite plainly regarded as not up to his own social level—'would accept my hospitality, too? I was thinking of reopening one of my houses here in the south before I enter into the commitments of matrimony, and also to enable Angela to see for herself what is in store for her. So what do you say to becoming my guests? For as long as I can persuade you to stay!'

'Not overlooking the fact that you are committed to marry Miss Grevil within the next five or six weeks,' Willow Ruddock reminded him.

'Of course!' For one fleeting second he looked as if his integrity had been called into question, and the slightly disdainful expression overspread his features once more ... but only for a very fleeting moment. 'I am not likely to forget such an obligation as that. My marriage is of supreme importance, but all the arrangements have already been concluded in connection with it. I am free to offer you such hospitality as will enable you to enjoy a more protracted holiday in Spain.'

'I must say I think that's terribly kind of you, *señor*,' the other woman member of the party leaned forward eagerly to assure him. She was thinking with relief that this would reduce her own and her husband's expenditure considerably. 'But I'm afraid we could only stay for a few days. We have to be back in London before the end of the month.'

'But I'm an entirely free agent,' Willow assured him, fluttering her remarkable eyelashes at him. 'And I adore Spain, as you know....'

'I do know.' He looked down at her with that soft light in his eyes Angela had never seen in them before. 'How about Mr. Hainsforth?' he enquired rather more coolly, indicating the only other male member of her entourage, apart from the Spaniards, who had not so far been consulted. 'Has he also to return to London before the end of the month, or is he a free agent as well?'

'Oh, Johnny's as free as I am, and he'd love to accept your invitation, wouldn't you, Johnny?' appealing to him by turning and touching his arm very lightly.

The Don's lips tightened.

'That is extremely gratifying, then,' he assured them both a trifle stiltedly. 'I shall look forward to the pleasure of your company at the Casa Martinez. This is an excellent arrangement we have arrived at, and all that remains is for me to assure myself that all is in readiness to receive you. Please supply me with the name of your hotel and I will have you collected from it at a day and time to be arranged.'

Mrs. Ruddock professed herself as delighted by the arrangement, her two married friends plainly regretted their inability to stay longer than a few days at the Casa, and Johnny Hainsforth looked neither pleased nor displeased. He was, in fact, an inoffensive-looking young man whom Angela strongly suspected was the type to be held in thrall by a sophisticated woman like Willow Ruddock, and he in his turn was the kind of willing admirer whom she probably liked to have in tow.

As for Angela, it was not until the others had departed that her fiancé remembered to enquire whether or not she thought it was a good thing to become a member of his house-party. He also informed her that he would, of course, consult her grandmother before taking it for granted that she would be permitted to join them, and while she was at the Casa Martinez she could inspect the present furnishings and equipment of the house and decide whether or not she would like extensive alterations made.

'I think your grandmother will approve of that,' he said, as if that was the only really important aspect of Angela's joining them.

Angela wished, for the first time in her life, that she had a very large circle of friends with one of whom she could stay—with her grandmother's blessing, of course—while Don Felipe was entertaining his friends.

As for the condition and contents of the Villa Martinez, she had no interest in them whatsoever, and was certainly not prepared to put him to the necessity of having the place refurnished for her. As far as she was concerned it was all part of a future that was entirely without any sort of appeal for her, and in fact she was beginning actively to resent the very thought of it.

To her own dismay she realised that she was in secret rebellion against it.

CHAPTER V

Don Felipe returned her to her grandmother's house at a respectable hour, and they didn't even wait to see the fireworks that were the one thing she might have enjoyed watching had she been asked. But following upon the somewhat abrupt departure of Mrs. Ruddock and her friends, who had remembered that they had other friends to meet with whom they were to watch the fireworks, Felipe seemed to lose interest in the evening altogether, and without even pretending that he wasn't bored by her unadulterated company suggested that she was probably feeling tired and would like to be taken home without delay.

Angela realised with a sense of curious shock that to her this was rather like the final straw. She had been forced to endure the society of his friends—one of whom was a woman who seemed to know him very well indeed, and whom he obviously and very openly admired—and the complete break-up of her evening, and he never even apologised for intruding his friends upon her, or affecting the quality of the evening.

And she strongly suspected from his decidedly marked silence on the drive home—quite a different kind of silence from the one that had engulfed him on the way to the hotel—that he was concentrating all his thoughts on Mrs. Ruddock, and probably making plans for her entertainment at the Casa.

She was even inclined to wonder whether her grandmother would approve the invitations he had issued that evening.

In the entrance to her grandmother's house he said his good-night. Absent-mindedly, almost, he bent his head over her hand and kissed it lightly, after expressing the formal hope that she would sleep well; and it was only when she practically snatched her hand away from him that he looked at her rather more attentively.

The mellow light from an antique lantern shone down upon her, and in her white dress she herself looked curiously pale and mutinous. Without looking at him she thanked him punctiliously.

'It was very kind of you to devote so much of your time to me this evening, *señor*. I have had a most diverting evening!'

She was about to dash away from him and into the house, where a light had been left burning dimly for her in the hall, but he declined to let go of her fingers and caught her back.

'Are you, perhaps, trying to convey to me that you have not enjoyed your evening?' he enquired in surprise.

She looked up at him in the diffused rays of the lantern, and her blue eyes sparkled coldly, like stars on a frosty night.

'What do you think, *señor*?' she returned bleakly. 'From my point of view, apart from the actual dinner with which you regaled me, was there very much that I could honestly claim to have enjoyed?'

He looked almost completely taken aback.

'But—but I thought——'

'You *thought, señor*? How often do you think seriously in connection with me? That I am a kind of willing tool, a useful appendage to have about the house now that you have made the decision to take me into your household? For treats I am to have ice-cream, and in front of your friends I can be referred to obliquely, as if I was not actually present, but never drawn into the conversation. I may give my assent, or dissent—if I dare to do so! But apart from that I must not have ideas, because even as Doña Angela Martinez my lot in life is to be severely circumscribed. Do you think, *señor*, that Mrs. *Ruddock* would ever be willing to fill such a rôle in *your* life?'

There was a moment of absolute silence between them, and then he threw back his head and laughed, and there was no doubt about it, he was honestly and intriguingly amused.

'Upon my word, little one, you can be a spitfire when you choose, can't you?' he said. He released her fingers, and his hand shifted to her chin, and he lifted it and looked down from his superior height with quite a noticeable degree of interest into her stormy eyes. 'You have a temper, which indicates that your Spanish blood has not been entirely swamped by your English blood, and apparently you have notions about yourself which were no doubt given strength at that Swiss school of yours. I must try and remember that you are not just as you appear on the surface.'

She wrenched away her chin, and her little teeth snapped together ... providing him with the impression that she might actually have bitten him had she found the courage.

'It has nothing to do with my school, *señor*,' she told him, in a muffled voice. 'I hope I have my father's family's pride!'

'Oho!' he exclaimed softly, as if still more amused. 'So it is your father's family who are responsible for this rebellion, is it? And what of your mother's family—Doña Miranda's family? Do they not also fill you with a sense of pride?'

'Of course, but it isn't the same....'

'You mean you want to be thought of as English?'

'If you like, yes!'

He regarded her almost quizzically, and trying to avoid the dark depths of his eyes she felt suddenly absurdly self-conscious, as if she had committed an actual breech of good behaviour and was regretting it already.

'And the English are not at all submissive, is that it?'

'I—I don't know much about the reactions of English women....'

'But you are one! You like to think of yourself as one!'

'I see no reason why I shouldn't, if it doesn't offend my grandmother....'

'Ah! You do do as your grandmother wishes you to do, don't you?'

He released her chin and fingered his own, smoothing the uncompromising jut of it with very thoughtful and shapely dark brown fingers.

'You were rebellious this afternoon, weren't you?' he said, remembering her hostility after the fitting of her wedding gown. 'So your attitude has nothing to do with Mrs. Ruddock, and that sudden eruption of her and her friends into the quiet of our little dinner together?'

'Of course not!' But she persisted in avoiding his eyes. 'However, since you mention her I might as well tell you, Don Felipe, that I do not think it would be a good thing if I added to the numbers of the house-party you are planning. For one thing, it is so close to our marriage that I have much to preoccupy me, and for another——'

'Yes?' he said, in that same soft tone that was almost silken in its softness, which vaguely irritated her because she more than suspected he was using it to mask his irritation with her, and his secret annoyance because she should all at once become so awkward to handle.

'I think it would be a mistake. We are not of the same world.'

'You mean she is not of your grandmother's

world?'

'I don't know.... No; no, it's not that! It's nothing at all to do with that!' She turned even more noticeably away from him, drooping her head a little, so that it looked rather like a bright flower wilting on a stem. 'But I don't think my grandmother would entirely approve.'

'Aha! You suspect some sort of a liaison between myself and Mrs. Ruddock? We have not always been such innocent friends, you would say...?'

She flung round swiftly to confront him, and for the second time that evening her innocuous English eyes flashed indignant Spanish sparks.

'You call her Carmelita!' she accused. 'She is not in the least like a Carmelita, and yet you call her by an absurd Spanish name! ... And it is very obvious, from the way in which you and she regard one another, and the delighted way in which you greeted one another, that your relationship has not always been very—very——'

'Distant?' he suggested, as if he wished to be helpful.

'Yes, distant!' Challengingly she met his eyes, and at the same time he could detect the fact that her slim breasts were heaving under the thin silk of her dress, and the muscles of her slender throat were quivering with a kind of righteous indignation. 'It is true she is a widow, and that you knew her husband, but one would never suspect that the real attachment was between you and the husband and not you and the wife after they had seen you together to-night!'

'Indeed,' he said, as if she had provided him with room for thought, 'that is most interesting.'

'And I'm sure my grandmother would have the same kind of feeling about Mrs. Ruddock that I—I have.'

'More than interesting,' he commented, as he plucked a sprig of jasmine from the wall and played with it between his fingers.

'Well?' she demanded, as if she meant to insist that he saw her point of view, but was by no means convinced he was treating the matter at all seriously. 'You do perfectly understand, *señor*, why I——'

'Why, no,' he admitted, smiling at her almost lazily and permitting her the gleam of his excellent white teeth in the glow of the overhead lantern, 'I cannot say that I "perfectly" understand. . . . But I do understand that you are lodging a protest. However, I can assure you that Doña Miranda will be most unlikely to raise any objections after I have had a talk with her tomorrow on the subject of your joining me and my friends at the Casa Martinez as soon as all the arrangements have been completed. She may not feel like chaperoning you herself, but there will be someone there to chaperone you . . . ignoring the fact that there will be other guests in the house. And of course it is important that you should be allowed to suggest your own improvements to the house. We shall quite possibly spend our honeymoon there, or at any rate a few weeks of it.'

'I have no improvements to suggest, *señor*,' she told him coldly.

'Dear me!' And his dark eyebrows quirked upwards. 'You do seem to have taken a dislike to the house in advance. Some people might consider that boded ill for the honeymoon I have just mentioned. However, you have not yet seen the Casa Martinez, or indeed any of my other houses, so perhaps you will be in for a pleasant surprise, and the honeymoon will be a success after all.'

'Good-night, *señor*,' she said, and turned away.

'Good-night, little one.... Though I do wish you would make it Felipe. Our married life is going to be very unusual if you insist on this formality. Altogether, I begin to suspect that, whatever happens, it will be unusual.'

She did not see the way in which he smiled as she moved determinedly away from him this time, and she was annoyed that he thought it necessary to open the outer door for her and make a careful inspection of the hall beyond it before permitting her to cross it on her way to the stairs.

'I shall see you tomorrow, Angela,' he said, as she stood waiting to put up the bolts for the night. 'I shall make it my business to see you after I have talked with your grandmother, and I feel certain I shall be able to reassure you about the complete wisdom of your becoming one of my guests at the Villa Martinez. And the next time I take you out I will try and remember that your tastes are a little

60

more sophisticated than I had imagined them to be, and we will cut out the ice-cream and substitute something more heady for your entertainment. Although I do not recollect that you even sipped the champagne that was provided for you this evening.'

'Only after your friends arrived, and you thought it necessary to order it,' Angela said to herself silently, as he turned his broad back to her and she watched his departure. And she tried to check the rising tide of resentment that, for some reason, was making her feel almost spiteful towards him—and most certainly Willow Ruddock—as she heard him running down the steps to his car.

Upstairs in her bedroom she removed the few items of jewellery she had worn that evening, and she slipped out of the white dress and thrust it out of sight in her wardrobe with the same intense dislike of it, that she had for everything connected with the evening just ended. It was beginning to perplex even herself before she finally slipped into her neatly turned-down bed.

The light extinguished, the moonlight flooded her room, bathing every item of furniture, and she tried to remember how brilliantly it had flooded over Don Felipe as he stood coping with her sudden rebellion outside in the courtyard where she had said her first good-night to him.

What an annoying man he was.... What an arrogant, assured, and in some ways unpredictable man. She had expected him to be annoyed, not amused, by her remarks about Mrs. Ruddock, but apparently they had amused him. And it was not enough to have the ability to amuse a man you were about to marry, and whose complete lifetime you were about to share. There had to be something more than that.... She felt uneasily sure of that.

Her grandmother might try and convince her that it was not so, and even her own common sense might tell her sometimes that she was fortunate to be marrying a man of stature and exemplary character who would look after her for the rest of her life, but the English half of her was absolutely certain that she was making a grave mistake.

It was not enough to look forward to a future and children, and no love ... just amiable affection and the knowledge that she could depend on the man she had married.

That evening she had seen his whole face light up when a pretty and charming woman climbed the steps of a hotel to meet him, and when she uninhibitedly put her hands into his and allowed him to hold on to them for such a length of time that it was an embarrassment to other people to look on at them.

What would it be like staying in his house, with him and Mrs. Ruddock, feeling absolutely certain in her heart that he admired her enormously?

And when a man admires a woman—a pretty woman!—and she is free, what is the net result? Does admiration mature, and with maturity do other ideas lift up their heads?

Angela felt absolutely certain that Mrs. Ruddock was no fool. She had seized upon the opportunity to extend her stay in Spain, and she hadn't even bothered to conceal the fact that she looked upon the Don's approaching marriage with amusement. She just didn't seriously believe that he was contemplating marriage!

And if he was contemplating marriage, then it was not the kind of marriage that troubled her very much.

At heart she was probably an adventuress, and she took such obstacles in her stride.

Angela had been uneasy and resentful earlier in the day, but after her evening's outing she found herself seething with resentment and indignation.

CHAPTER VI

VERY much to Angela's surprise Doña Miranda seemed to think there was nothing odd about Don Felipe wishing to entertain a few of his friends at one of his houses before finally parting with his freedom as a bachelor. And she immediately sanctioned her granddaughter's acceptance of the invitation he had issued to her to become one of his guests. But she insisted that she herself should accompany Angela as her *duenna*, and when the girl sought to make acceptance of the invitation impossible by pointing out that the elderly woman would find it exhausting, pooh-poohed the idea as absolute nonsense.

'I shall love it,' she declared. 'I'm quite fond of Felipe, as you know, and I've heard a great deal about his houses. I believe the Casa Martinez is filled with some very fine furniture—paintings, and that sort of thing, you know. Felipe's grandfather collected them, and of all his homes he liked the Casa best. In fact, he died there.... Perhaps that is one reason why Felipe has avoided it since it came into his possession. It needs a young family to give it fresh life, and once you are married it will be a part of your duty to supply that need. And in the meantime you can make up your mind about fresh hangings, and that sort of thing. I'm sure Felipe will give you *carte blanche* to buy whatever you wish, and I shall thoroughly enjoy advising you.'

She looked as if she meant to enjoy the visit in any case, and despite the fact that she could seldom summon up the energy to travel anywhere, and a visit to her solicitor in Madrid was the one event in the year for which she planned weeks ahead, began immediately to examine the contents of her own wardrobe, and advised her granddaughter to pack some really charming clothes for the visit.

'If there are to be other women amongst the guests you must not allow them to outshine you,' she said. 'And you have recently acquired so many pretty new things that it will not seriously deplete your trousseau if you select some of them to wear on this visit.'

'But why...?' Angela wanted to enquire—with a certain amount of reason. For Don Felipe was committed to marry her, and it was not a question of her having to put herself out to please him and attract him.

However, she took her grandmother's advice and made a careful selection from amongst her new clothes. She had to admit that it gave her a certain amount of pleasure, and to her own astonishment she felt suddenly determined—and it was a matter of almost vital importance—that Mrs. Ruddock, with her willowy golden beauty, should not cast her into the shade by wearing smarter or more elegantly styled garments. She might wear more spectacular ones, but Doña Miranda had footed the bill for a trousseau that was quite exquisite, and as Angela ran her finger over supple silks and shimmering hand-embroidered satins she knew that she could feel confident whatever she wore.

In particular, she delighted in an apple green evening gown with crystal embroidery, and a white watered silk that stood out about her slender legs and ankles like a board. It, too, had some skilful embroidery, and the shoes that were intended to be worn with it had brocaded roses on their insteps, and at the heart and centre of each rose was a large crystal drop.

Happily, too, she had plenty of attractive day clothes, and for the journey to the Casa she wore a tailored silk dress in a heavenly shade of clear azure blue. She wore dark glasses and no hat, and the Don, when he called for her and her grandmother in a silver-grey Bentley that was sufficiently commodious to ensure that Doña Miranda travelled smoothly and with the maximum amount of comfort, frowned at the sight of her unprotected golden head, particularly as the sun was very hot.

'You should wear a hat,' he told her. 'With hair like that you should take care to avoid the effects of too much sun.'

She smiled at him carelessly. She might be fair, but she could stand any amount of sun.

'I dislike hats,' she replied. 'Whenever I can I dispense with one.'

At that he frowned more forbiddingly than before.

'It is more ladylike to wear a hat,' he informed her in the bleak tones of pronounced disapproval. 'And gloves, too,' he added, observing that her grandmother, making herself comfortable in the back of the car, was meticulously hatted and gloved. 'Ask Doña Miranda if a young woman about to acquire the responsibilities and obligations of marriage should not appear more formally in public.'

She could not be absolutely certain that he was entirely serious, but her grandmother failed to overhear the interchange, and she decided to ignore his suggestion. She accepted a seat beside him in the front of the car, and they moved away from the villa and off along the blinding white-hot road to the Casa Martinez.

The Casa Martinez was very near the sea, and the heat of the sun was tempered by the cool airs from the sea before they actually reached it. Doña Miranda stared at the heaving, brilliantly blue expanse of ocean with detached eyes, for she had never sunbathed on a beach or entered the water in a swimsuit in the whole of her life, and she knew she was quite unlikely to begin to do so at her time of life, or in the station of life to which she most fortunately belonged by birth. But Angela had brought a swimsuit with her, and she had no doubt Willow Ruddock spent the better part of her life on sunlit beaches like this—in between skiing in

Switzerland and decorating the Casino at Monte Carlo.

The house itself stood surrounded by splendidly kept grounds, and although it had a turn-of-the-century ungainliness about it, the exterior suggested that the interior was very opulent. It had been originally intended as a summer residence for members of the Martinez family, and it was spacious enough to accommodate large numbers of them and their friends. It was blazingly white, with cool green shutters and pantiled roofs, and from every window in the front of the house there were spectacular views of the sea and the yellow shelving beach.

The car came to rest in a quiet inner courtyard where the walls were covered in flaming growth, and a fountain played in a marble basin and added to the beneficent sense of coolness that the nearness to the sea had already affected it with. Through an archway Angela could see the gardens falling away in terraces, and amongst other bewildering perfumes she actually caught the scent of roses.

'Well?' Don Felipe glanced at her as he helped her alight. 'This is as you imagined it? Or perhaps more attractive than you imagined it?'

'It is very nice, yes,' Angela agreed, but with a deliberate restraint which told him that she was not prepared to go into ecstasies about anything connected with him, despite the fact that it had all been arranged that she should marry him.

He shrugged his white-clad shoulders. She had

68

the feeling that he was annoyed, and his mellow mood of the night before had entirely forsaken him.

He helped Doña Miranda to alight as if her bones were very fragile indeed, and she, at least, he knew would appreciate his solicitude. And on her way into the house she paused to admire various features of it on the outside which quite obviously pleased him, and when he transferred his attention once more to his fiancée there was a certain asperity about both his look and his tone.

'My other guests have not arrived yet, but you must feel free to move about the house as you will. But first I am sure you will wish to be shown to your rooms.'

A middle-aged, dark-eyed housekeeper, Señora Cortez, showed them to their rooms. Angela's had balconies overlooking the well-tended lawns in front of the house, but Doña Miranda had been permitted an excellent view of the sea. As she was unlikely to make trips to it or spend any time on the shore enjoying the health-giving ozone this was some compensation for what she would otherwise be missing during her visit. She could spend the coolest hours of every day on her balcony, relaxing in a specially constructed and superbly comfortable chair with a book or her writing materials, and, as a matter of fact, expressed every intention of doing so.

Both rooms were very comfortably if somewhat severely furnished, and already Doña Miranda was casting her eyes around and taking mental notes of deficiencies. She was confident that she and her granddaughter were going to have an entertaining time listing improvements and discussing such things as furnishing fabrics and possible innovations, and although Angela was not looking forward to this diversion with the same amount of enthusiasm as her grandmother she was interested from the outset in the queer dignity and old Spanish charm of the Casa Martinez.

She liked the cool white walls and the dark Spanish oak that contrasted so attractively with them, the handsome chests and solid furniture with which the place was filled. She couldn't imagine modern furnishings looking half as well, and certainly nothing could replace the rows and rows of portraits in solid ornamental frames that were a visual record of the Martinez family. As soon as she had changed for lunch and repaired the slight ravages to her make-up that had been caused by the journey, she wandered in the gallery on to which the door of her room opened and studied face after face as it looked down at her. She had already arrived at the conclusion that for the most part Martinez men and women were a little forbidding of aspect, and certainly extremely dark in the best tradition of their Latin forebears; and only here and there could she discover a Martinez as handsome as Don Felipe, when she heard him coming along the gallery behind her, and he joined her in front of the portrait of one of his great-uncles.

'Ah,' he exclaimed, as he looked her up and down with approval—he, too, had changed into one of his thin tussore suits that became him so well, and looked as if he had just emerged from a shower, he was so composed and cool—'I see you are making acquaintance with some of my ancestors. You will find more of them in Madrid, at my principal home, but these are pretty representative. I've no doubt the English half of you finds them rather alarming, but you needn't really have any fear of your future in-laws ... my uncles are all extremely amiable, particularly my Uncle José, whom you may meet during this visit, and my numerous cousins and aunts seem pretty harmless to me. Once you are a member of the family I'm sure they will put themselves out to make you really feel one of us.'

'Thank you.' She sounded a little dry. Surely, she thought, after her most recent conversations with him, he could not surely imagine she was anxious to be made one with other members of his family?

He was in an obviously better humour than when he had collected her and her grandmother that morning, and even slightly expansive.

'As soon as we are married,' he said to her, 'we must have your portrait painted, too, and you can hang amongst the rest——' He waved a hand to indicate the watchful row of faces. 'That will give you a feeling of belonging.'

'Thank you,' she said again, even more drily.

His appreciative eyes were taking in the warm

beauty of her hair in the dimness of the gallery, and the slender grace of her figure in the cool, apple-green linen into which she had recently changed. She was all white and gold, he reflected ... and it would be a change from that slightly sinister sable quality that looked out of most of the portraits.

'By the way,' he remarked, as he helped himself to a cigarette from his case and tapped it on the back of one of his shapely fingernails, 'I am having some flowers sent to your room. They should have been there to greet you on your arrival, but apparently Señora Cortez slipped up.'

'Oh!' she exclaimed, as if this was a contingency she had not anticipated. So far he had sent her flowers on two occasions, but they had come straight from a florist's, and he had probably never seen them. On this occasion they were almost certainly to be an offering from his garden, and it would appear he was concerning himself with how soon she received them.

'How lovely!' she exclaimed automatically. 'I have already noticed that you have many flowers in the garden.'

'But these are rather special roses—red roses. My gardener dislikes cutting them, and I believe it affects him adversely when he does so on my order.'

'Oh!' she exclaimed again, and wondered how often when visiting the Casa Martinez he ordered the cutting of red roses either for the decoration of the house or for one of his guests. She suspected he did not concern himself with the decoration of the house, so therefore it was probably a favoured guest who received them.

Without entirely understanding why she did so, or recognising the quality of the link-up, she asked:

'How soon will Mrs. Ruddock and her friends be arriving? I suppose they did, after all, accept your invitation?'

'Oh yes.' But the dryness had suddenly transferred itself to his tone, and a rather peculiar look entered his eyes as they rested upon her. 'They will be here before evening.'

'Mrs. Ruddock appears to travel a good deal.'

'Yes; I believe she does.'

'I don't quite understand how she manages to do it when English people have to make do with a travel allowance. She is fortunate to have friends like you when she visits Spain. Perhaps she has similar friends in other countries.'

'Perhaps,' he agreed, almost urbanely.

She shot him a look that was a mixture of suspicion and faint, uncontrollable irritation.

'Does she also like red roses, *señor*?'

'I believe so.... Although on the occasion of her visit this time I have ordered yellow ones for her room. She is rather like a yellow rose—or a golden orchid!—herself, don't you think?'

Angela bit her lip and did not answer. She realised she had asked for that.

She accompanied him downstairs to the cool,

flagged hall, and then he led the way to the main sitting-room, or *sala*, and asked her whether she would like a glass of sherry before accompanying him into the dining-room. With great regret Doña Miranda, who took her duties as *duenna* very seriously despite the fact that the two were engaged to be married—perhaps, she would have explained, because of it—had been forced to refuse to join them at lunch, the unaccustomed exertions of the journey and the preparation for it beforehand having tired her very much, and she had had to request the housekeeper to take a tray to her room. After that she proposed to rest, and was quite sure she would be fit to join them in the evening.

So Angela and her fiancé lunched alone in the dim and impressive dining-room, he occupying the head of a long and gleaming table while she sat demurely at his right hand. The table was laid as if for an important occasion with fine lace table mats and sheerest crystal, gleaming silver, fruit and flowers. Angela was glad she hadn't been placed at the opposite end of the table, and then reflected that as she was not yet mistress of the house this would have been incorrect.

And that set another thought moving through her head.

When Mrs. Ruddock arrived, would she be given the place of honour at the host's right hand, or would that still be reserved for his fiancée?

It was not a particularly sparkling meal, with lively conversation seldom flagging for a moment, for Angela was by no means at her ease lunching under such conditions. She found it a taxing experience dining with him in a restaurant, where there was music to divert them, and other people around them; but here, in his own house, with him acting the part of thoughtful and attentive host, it was almost too much.

Although she kept her eyes almost permanently lowered throughout the meal, she had the feeling that he watched her openly on occasion, and that there was rather unkind amusement in his eyes. He knew she was not enjoying herself—not even the excellent and varied dishes that were carried to the table from the side-table—and he also knew she was not making the smallest effort to be an entertaining guest—or fiancée, if it came to that. And he also knew she was brooding on the thought of the arrival of Mrs. Ruddock and her friends, and that brought an inscrutable look into his eyes.

'Such a pity I did not order champagne,' he murmured, since she declined resolutely to sample any of the wines and stuck to her English favourite, a cool fruit drink. 'But there will be champagne to-night, when Mrs. Ruddock is here!'

While she was pouring out coffee for him at the dining-table, she couldn't refrain from giving her curiosity a little ventilation.

'Why do you call her Carmelita?' she asked.

He smiled.

'Didn't you ask me that before?'

'I said that I thought it was rather an absurd

name for someone who is not in the least Spanish. I don't think I actually asked you why you call her Carmelita.'

Without her asking him to do so he selected and pared for her a gloriously ripe peach from the fruit bowl, and set it on her plate in front of her before he made the least attempt to satisfy her curiosity.

'It somehow suits her. I cannot tell you why, but to me Willow does not suit her half so well. What do you think?' he enquired conversationally, as he started to prepare a peach for himself.

'I think both names are—theatrical. She is certainly tall and willowy, and therefore Willow is perhaps quite a good name for her; but as I am half Spanish myself I don't like to hear her called by such a name as Carmelita.'

'Ah!' he exclaimed, as if she had thrown light on something that had previously puzzled him. 'So you do, after all, acknowledge that you have some Spanish blood, and it is a fact that that blood, which is not shared by Mrs. Ruddock, resents having some Spanish quality bestowed on her. Well, in deference to your feelings in this matter, I will, while she is here, call her Willow—if that will make you happier. I can keep the Carmelita for occasions when you are not present and your ear is unlikely to be offended!'

Angela lifted indignant white eyelids and stared directly at him. She thought that he smiled coolly, with the blandest form of amusement; and then, as the meal was ended, suggested she retired to her room for a siesta.

'Perhaps after tea I will take you for a bathe,' he said, 'although on the whole it might be better if you wait until morning, as I can't have you collecting heat-stroke. The mornings—the very early mornings—are deliciously cool on this coast, and I think you will find a bathe invigorating then. Besides, your grandmother might approve more if the other members of the party are with us. I happen to be aware that Doña Miranda is a great stickler for what she believes to be correct.'

Doña Miranda's granddaughter was very well aware of this, too, but at the same time she thought that a bathe in the cool of the evening would have been delightful. Thinking the matter over while she rested in her room, the green sun-blinds only partially drawn over the open windows because she disliked to be enclosed, and the Spanish method of sealing oneself in in the heat of the day did not appeal to her at all, she decided that she could steal out by herself after tea and make her way down to the beach, with those enchanting deep mauve and emerald green rocks littering it, like monsters on an alien shore, and have a bathe all by herself, without anyone being aware of it.

She was a strong swimmer, and it seemed absurd to be within actual hailing distance of the sea and not actually in it. The heat was certainly intense outside the windows, and the gardens positively swam in the violent ultra-white light. She marvelled that such things as roses flourished out there

in that brazen glare, and turned to look at the
enormous vase of gorgeous, heavily scented dark
red roses that had found their way to her room
while she was lunching with Felipe. She wondered
whether the same person who had borne them to
her room had also carried a similar vase of yellow
roses to Mrs. Ruddock's room, and had considered
that the distinction between a fiancée and a guest
was not being exactly over-emphasised. It was true
that red roses had a particular significance in some
people's minds, but others preferred yellow ones.
Therefore, it was simply a matter of preference....

She exerted herself in the afternoon heat to walk
across the room and detach one of the red roses
from the vase, and she inhaled the perfume of it
thoughtfully for several seconds. Then she replaced
it in the water, just as thoughtfully. She was not
herself able to make up her mind about her own
preference for red or yellow roses.... But at least
these were particularly splendid specimens.

She supposed she must thank Felipe politely for
them when she saw him again.

She decided to postpone her first bathe in the
enticing blue sea that so tempted her whenever she
set foot on her balcony, at any rate until the following day, and went along to see her grandmother
when she felt reasonably certain her rest period was
over. Doña Miranda was sipping tea with lemon
when she entered her room, and although every
chink of sunlight was rigorously excluded from the
room as if it was a very dangerous enemy the

dimness inside the handsomely furnished apartment was rather pleasant, and in it Angela could see that her grandmother was completely rested.

'Ah, child,' she exclaimed, as Angela closed the door, 'I was thinking about you just now, and wondering what you are going to wear to-night.'

Angela shrugged her shoulders slightly.

'Does it matter?' she asked. 'All my clothes are new and attractive, and it might be the simplest method of making a choice if I just run my hand along the row inside the wardrobe and pick out the one I grasp hold of first.'

Doña Miranda looked noticeably irritated.

'Child,' she reproved her, 'there are moments when I despair of you! You are about to be married to a most attractive man, and yet you think it is quite unnecessary to do anything at all to please him. Don't you feel in the slightest degree flattered that he has selected you for his bride?'

'No,' Angela answered, and sat down on the side of her grandmother's bed while she smiled at her engagingly to make up for the apparent ungraciousness of her answer.

Doña Miranda looked at her long and critically.

'You think the advantages are all on his side?'

'I only know that I did not ask him to marry me, and I would be quite content if he suddenly released me from the engagement, and I could contemplate marrying someone else—when I felt like marrying someone else!' she added provokingly.

Her grandmother frowned very blackly at this.

'That is the sort of thing I certainly do not like to hear you say,' she replied coldly. 'For one thing, it is most unfair to the man you are to marry, and for another ...' She broke off, as the sound of a car entering the courtyard below reached her ears. 'The other guests?' she enquired, her alert glance following her granddaughter as the girl moved sinuously to the window and peered through the slats of the closed shutters into the courtyard below. 'They have arrived, yes?'

'They have arrived, yes,' Angela answered.

Doña Miranda spoke briskly.

'Wear the white watered silk to-night, Angela, and the pearls I gave you on your last birthday. Take particular pains with your appearance to-night, if only to please me. Is that understood? ... I wish it!'

'Of course.' Angela smiled at her as if she was humouring her, could think of no real reason why she shouldn't humour her grandmother in this respect, and then made for the door and her own room.

A maid was in the bathroom running a bath for her, and she herself lifted the white watered silk out of the wardrobe. She took all the necessary pains to ensure that, when she finally stood before her mirror and recognised that she was ready, and that there was virtually nothing more she could do to herself that would improve the reflection given

80

back to her from the mirror, her grandmother would be satisfied when she saw her. And far from wishing to please Don Felipe it never even occurred to her to wonder whether he liked her in white, or whether he might be of the opinion that she wore too much of it, and that it had the effect of rendering her slightly insipid.

She delayed so long over her toilet that by the time she descended to the ground floor of the villa the others were all in the main *sala*, and being regaled with sherry and more potent refreshment. Her grandmother was ensconced in the seat of honour at the elbow of the host, and Mrs. Ruddock was standing in the middle of a beautiful Oriental rug and declaring that the colours in it were quite perfect. She was apparently an expert on Oriental rugs, as well as china and glass, and everything in the long, cool room appeared to delight her.

Angela was glad, as soon as her eye alighted on her, that she hadn't worn her apple green dress with the crystal embroidery, for Willow Ruddock was wearing a daring shade of emerald green, and about her slender throat was a quite spectacular diamond necklace. In order to attract attention to the latter she toyed with it carelessly with the tips of her shapely white fingers, and each movement of her hands also drew attention to the matching bracelets she wore on her graceful wrists, and if this display of collateral was anything to go by she had no need, when and if she contemplated remarrying, to marry a man for his worldly wealth and any personal advantages of that sort.

It was quite plain that she was very well endowed as it was.

Johnny Hainsforth, who had been following in her shadow in a most devoted way on the occasion that Angela had first met her in Granada, was also occupying the middle of the Oriental rug, and in that way standing as close to her as he could get, and her two other friends had also accompanied her. It was quite clear that they had considered it beyond their powers to turn down this invitation, and Angela gathered that they were prepared to stay for at least a week if their host could put up with them for that length of time.

Doña Miranda looked down her aristocratic nose at them, as if she recognised them immediately as nothing to do with her world, but the appearance of Mrs. Ruddock seemed to interest and even intrigue her. She condescended to put a few rather leading questions to Willow, and when she discovered that the widow spoke Spanish, conversed with her for a short while in that tongue, although she quickly reverted to English either because it was less exhausting for her personally, or as an act of politeness which she felt was demanded of her.

Angela managed to slip quietly into the room without anyone save her grandmother noticing her until she had actually been standing beside one of the windows for a full minute, and then she declined anything to drink when Felipe sought to put a glass of sherry into her hand.

At the same time his eyes roved over her without revealing either interest, appreciation or criticism —which was virtually impossible, anyway, since she looked very youthful, slender, and as fresh as a half-opened white rosebud.

'You are late,' he commented. 'I was beginning to wonder whether or not you intended to join us.'

Angela both looked and felt surprised.

'I have been standing here for nearly a minute,' she said. 'I didn't think you noticed me.'

He glanced at his watch.

'Exactly forty-five seconds,' he said. 'And I noticed you the instant you appeared in the doorway.'

Angela had been speculating considerably about the possible seating arrangements at dinner, but it certainly surprised her when she found she was given the place of honour at his right hand, while Mrs. Ruddock was relegated to his left hand. Doña Miranda was asked if she would occupy the seat at the foot of the table opposite his own, and this recognition that she was temporarily fulfilling the position of hostess seemed to please her.

It put her in a good mood for the long-drawn-out meal that followed, and Mrs. Ruddock and her three companions received somewhat kinder treatment from her than they might otherwise have done. Angela did not need to be told that her grandmother was resenting their inclusion in the party largely because Mrs. Ruddock was so exceptionally personable, and with the knowledge that her granddaughter was about to contract a matrimonial alliance with the man who had invited her this made Doña Miranda just a little wary. She had no reason whatever to suspect the absolute integrity of Don Felipe Martinez, and his family background rendered it impossible for him to do anything that would cause any single one of his numerous relatives to elevate so much as a corner of an eyebrow.

But she was sufficiently worldly-wise to acknowledge that a man was, after all, a man, and the very fact that he continued a friendship with such a one as Willow Ruddock, *after* the death of her husband who could have been the main reason for the friendship in the first place, was a circumstance which might have been viewed with suspicion had anyone other than Don Felipe been involved. But the fact that it was Don Felipe, and her future grandson-in-law, lulled all suspicions.

She had, however, been conscious of a distinct sensation of shock when Mrs. Ruddock was first presented to her, and she felt vexed with Angela for not making it absolutely clear that the woman was an adventuress. She must be an adventuress or she would not accept invitations from men like Don Felipe when they had just announced their intention of marrying.

If only Angela, who was ridiculously reticent,

had talked more about the quality of her looks, and more important even than her looks her faintly challenging air of looking upon the world as her oyster, and old-fashioned martinets like Doña Miranda rather amusing.... Well, she might have had something to say to her future grandson-in-law before they left for the Casa Martinez. But now that they were here it would be bad taste, and most insulting to the host, to behave as if she was already looking askance at his old friend's widow, and therefore she sought to appear more affable than she was actually far from feeling.

She led the conversation at dinner into channels that could offend no one, and put no great strain on the English visitors, who were, after all, virtual strangers to Spain and must not be given a bad impression of it. But afterwards she saw to it that it was Angela who poured out coffee in the *sala*—and, incidentally, did it very gracefully and composedly and in a way that reflected excellently on her Swiss finishing school. And she also saw to it that Angela could not possibly be ignored by thrusting her into the midst of the others by the simple expedient of requesting her to relate certain stories of Spanish folk-lore for the benefit of the strangers, while Don Felipe looked on in faint but obvious amusement because Angela obeyed her grandmother's commands so readily, while plainly having little relish for the prominence that was thus thrust on her.

Nevertheless, she acquitted herself very well, while her voice was so clear and attractive and

English that he actually found himself listening quite attentively for any repetition of its various cadences.

Mrs. Ruddock could not have looked more bored, but she strove to conceal it occasionally by smiling at Angela in an indulgent fashion. Johnny Hainsforth, although only too plainly a lifelong admirer of Willow, also regarded Angela with admiration, which was sufficiently discreet to cause no offence to her fiancé; and the other two guests spent the evening exclaiming delightedly over the various magnificent antiques with which the Casa Martinez was filled.

Angela went to bed when her grandmother retired, and she had no knowledge of how soon the others sought the comfort of their high Spanish beds.

She knew that Mrs. Ruddock smiled still more indulgently when the autocratic voice of Doña Miranda insisted that the bride-to-be had had a sufficiently long day and should be glad to retire, and there was no concealing the incredulous amusement in Willow's smoky-grey eyes when the host simply bent and saluted the girl's finger-tips with courtly grace before wishing her a perfectly cool good-night.

Even Johnny Hainsforth looked surprised, as also did the other two guests, who were striving to behave in a manner they felt was expected of them. But plainly everyone was struck by the inescapable fact that Don Felipe and the girl who was shortly to become Doña Felipe were as good as strangers in their attitudes to one another.

If anything happened to prevent the marriage neither of them would be acutely distressed.

CHAPTER VII

ANGELA went to bed resenting the fact that she had been placed in an impossible position. She didn't blame her grandmother, but she did blame herself for being such a disgrace to her father's memory as to submit without any effective protest.

She remained awake for half the night in the strange, cool room that struck her as extraordinarily inhospitable, and awoke with the sunrise to the decision that she took at the moment of waking that she would make her way down to the beach and enjoy her first bathe in the limpid sea while nobody else was up and about.

It was such a glorious morning that for a short while her cares and her resentments melted away as she floated and struck out in a leisurely manner in the water that felt like sun-warmed silk. She had bought herself a white bathing-suit before she left and it suited her admirably, particularly as she wore no cap and her warm golden hair floated out behind her on the water. She decided she had plenty of time to dry it and then shampoo it before breakfast, and as she always set it herself there would be no disadvantage to her immersing it in this manner.

And she needn't join the others until after

breakfast. She and her grandmother always breakfasted in their rooms when they were at home, and
she saw no reason to change her habits because she
was the guest of her fiancé.

This was a magnificent stretch of coast, and not
for the first time pride of race stirred in her breast.
Only this time it was pride of being Spanish—with
all this flamboyant beauty a part of her heritage.

She emerged from the water at the moment
when the heat of the sun climbing into the brilliant arc of blue sky was beginning to make itself
felt a little unpleasantly, and the indigo patches of
shade attached to the lavender rocks was almost
painfully accented in contrast with the shimmering
pale gold beach. She could see the Casa rising
above her, and as she walked towards it she also
made out a group of people emerging from it, and
amongst them was Willow Ruddock in—of all
things—a bikini, which would probably shock
Doña Miranda to the core of her being if she was
permitted to catch so much as a glimpse of it. The
host was wearing bathing-trunks and looking
splendidly fit and brown, and as it was the first
time Angela had seen him without the benefit of the
most formal attire she felt wildly and uncomfortably
that she had to avert her eyes not only from Don
Felipe, but from the other two men who were
similarly sketchily attired.

She herself had brought a terry towelling wrap
to cover her own modest swimsuit during the journey to and from the house—just in case she en-

countered anyone on the way—and she was clutching at it with her hands and holding it close around her when she unavoidably bumped into the others.

She heard Willow Ruddock laugh, and then the other woman stopped and pointed directly at her with a shapely derisive finger.

'My dear, aren't you absolutely *cooking*?' she demanded. 'I know you Spanish have a thing about respectability, but this is carrying things to extremes! Felipe, are you going to insist that your wife goes into a sort of purdah when you marry her, or has she somehow got hold of the notion that you are?'

She was so strikingly beautiful in her own brief bikini that was the same colour as the frock she had worn the night before that for a few seconds Angela stared at her in admiration, and then the realisation that she was being made fun of by the other girl, who was her fiancé's guest, brought a flush of scarlet to her face. Far from releasing her hold on her protective robe she clutched at it more tightly, and instead of seeing—after those few seconds of pure envy—an extraordinarily beautiful and, in fact, rather gorgeous girl, who resembled in a way a gorgeous piece of horseflesh, she saw confronting her an extremely malicious young woman of an alien race who was determined to belittle her if she could.

But Felipe, with an expression that was almost one of outrage, defended his fiancée to his guest.

'Angela is simply behaving in the way she was

brought up,' he explained with acid curtness. 'In Spain we do not believe that the shop window is the place for all the finest wares ... quite the contrary, in fact!' Then, more sharply to Angela: 'Go on up to the house, *querida*, and change into something more suitable. No doubt you will be breakfasting with your grandmother.'

It was dismissal, but Angela did not mind. For the first time in her life she was grateful for the fact that he had the right to order her about, and although the others appealed to her to join them, and Willow looked taken aback—even a little vexed with herself for a moment—she did not pause to question his right to be so authoritative before they were even married. As she sped on up to the house it did occur to her that the incident that had just ended was a guideline of the way he might behave to her in the future, but for once such a thought did not trouble her.

He might be planning to order her life for her, but he could defend his own. Willow Ruddock had actually looked confused ... and that pleased her.

Later in the day she met them all again when they had returned from the beach, and Willow was dressed in an immaculate sun-suit, and even looked rather demure, for she had chosen one that could cause offence to no one, and was even a little in the mode of Angela's own dresses. She was seated beneath a sun-umbrella on the terrace that overlooked the sloping lawns and the pergolas of roses, and although she wore dark glasses the eyes behind them were engagingly frank. She beckoned with a finger as Angela approached along the terrace, and said that she wanted to apologise for her conduct on the beach that morning.

'I'm afraid I was indiscreet and said something to which Felipe took exception,' she confessed, at the same time accepting a long, cool drink from a servant who also appeared on the terrace with a tray of refreshments. 'Ah, lots of ice!' she exclaimed, beaming upwards at the dark face of the servant. 'Just the way I like it, in fact!'

The servant withdrew, and she continued addressing Angela:

'You mustn't take any notice if I'm a bit brash at times. I was brought up very differently from you, you know, and I'm also quite a few years older, and it struck me you might be in for a raw deal unless you stick up for yourself rather more forcibly on occasion. This morning you should not have allowed Felipe to dismiss you as he did.'

Angela, who was also sipping a lemonade, shrugged her slender shoulders.

'I was not aware that Felipe dismissed me,' she lied with dignity.

Mrs. Ruddock smiled at her.

'Oh, come now.... He ordered you back to the house to change. Has he ever seen you in a swimsuit?'

'Never.'

'Then he is in for a treat, because I was watching you from my window while you were enjoying your solitary bathe, and I must say you've got a most attractive figure, and as a matter of fact that prim little outfit you had on this morning suits you. And you are a very strong swimmer. Does he know that?'

'Not so far as I am aware.'

Another faint smile curved the attractive shape of Willow Ruddock's lips.

'How formally you talk ... rather like a book of etiquette designed for an old-fashioned school for very old-fashioned young ladies. Does your grandmother insist that you behave formally? Have you been brought up like that?'

'I have been brought up to conform to a set of rules.'

'Mostly obsolete these days in England and America, where young people are all for freedom. How do you, being partly English, regard freedom? I mean, does it worry you that you are so much hampered by tradition, and all that sort of thing?'

'Not in the least.'

This was not, perhaps, strictly true, but she said it as if she had no reservations whatsoever.

Willow looked at her rather hard for a moment, the large sun-glasses she wore concealing much of the staggering beauty of her eyes and her astonishing eyelashes, while at the same time they succeeded in emphasising the purity of her complexion and the sheer skill of her make-up. Then she shrugged her shoulders as if she felt she was up against an unfamiliar problem.

'I'm afraid I haven't met many young women like you, certainly not young women who live under the domination of a grandmother and are prepared to submit to the same sort of domination when they become wives. And you are not anticipating altering the form at all when you're Señora Martinez, are you?' she stated rather than asked. 'I mean, you'll go on ... just submitting? There won't be any attempt made to assert yourself? All your life you'll be a kind of shadow walking in the footsteps of Felipe? Which seems to me fantastic in this day and age!'

It was Angela's turn to smile slightly at her.

'My marriage has been arranged,' she confessed, 'but I am quite looking forward to leading a different life once I marry. I shall, for instance, be my own mistress, in charge of my own house—Felipe's house, too, of course!—and there will be many new and interesting things to occupy me. It will be very different from living with my grandmother!'

'I should hope so!' Willow drawled.

Angela felt it necessary to amplify her position:

'To you arranged marriages must seem strange, but then you have no Spanish blood. And very few Spanish women are actively unhappy once they marry.... Perhaps it is because they are easily made content. I am half English, but basically I think I'm very Spanish....' Whether this was true or not she herself could not be quite sure, but from the way her little chin jutted she wished it to be clearly understood that she had few if any doubts on this head. 'Yes, I'm sure I'm *very* Spanish!' she emphasised.

Mrs. Ruddock looked both amused and sceptical.

'To me you look *very* English. But I don't doubt your grandmother, who I gather has had complete charge of you since you were very small, has seen to it that the importance of being Spanish has been underlined many, many times since you were first able to understand what she was talking about. However, you do intrigue me a little ... perhaps because you look so English. And I happen to believe I know Felipe rather well, and I was honestly absolutely amazed when he said he was going to marry you. You see, if Felipe marries he ought to marry someone who will dominate rather than submit to him.... I think he could be rather cruel if he thought a woman was his slave. If she made *him her* slave, on the other hand, it would bring out the best in him. I am as certain of that as I am that spring follows winter, even in a country like this.'

Angela regarded her as if she was by no means certain of what she was getting at.

'And that being the case...?' she suggested tentatively.

'Unless you assert yourself you're likely to become his slave, and in ten years' time I wouldn't like to think how badly crushed you'd be. Of course, if you're madly in love with Felipe I suppose it's all right, but you don't look to me as if you've ever been in love with anyone. You have a completely unawakened look.'

Angela hesitated. She saw no reason why she should uncover her soul for the benefit of Mrs. Ruddock, but she was truthful by nature and also by upbringing, and after a pause she heard herself admitting, while she stared into the dregs of her lemonade:

'I have never been in love with anyone. I am not quite sure I understand what "being in love" means.'

'Then you most certainly should not marry Felipe!'

'No?' The clear, sea-blue eyes were lifted and gazed straight at the dark glasses confronting her. 'But is it not possible I may yet fall "in love" with Felipe?'

'Not if you have not already done so!'

'You do not think it is at all possible that he is in love with me?'

Willow lighted herself a cigarette, which she selected from a neat platinum case inset with her own initials in diamonds, and shook her head—and laughed pityingly.

'My poor child,' she said, 'you are not entertaining delusions on that score, are you?'

Angela continued to regard her unabashed.

'You do not think he is the least little bit in love with me, Mrs. Ruddock?'

Another shake of the head answered her.

'Yet you do think it is not impossible that he

should fall in love? With someone else?'

Willow tried to look vaguely uncomfortable, and then she removed the dark glasses, bent forward and laid a hand over Angela's, where it rested on the round table top.

'My poor child,' she repeated, 'you have no knowledge of Felipe whatsoever, have you? No real knowledge! This marriage has been thrust upon you and in a matter of weeks you are going to find yourself tied to a man who is a virtual stranger to you. To me that sounds absolutely horrible! ... Believe me, it does! For I do know Felipe, and I—I——'

'*You* are not in love with him, Mrs. Ruddock,' with a dryness and conviction that quite shook the older woman. 'If you are it is not the sort of love that could be of very great value to him. But you do strongly suspect that he is in love with you? For a long time, perhaps?'

Willow shrugged her shoulders helplessly.

'I have said that I think that being in love with a woman could transform him, and if Felipe married me I could transform him. Instead of the self-centred, egotistical male you see now there would be someone very, very different, I assure you.' She flicked ash from her cigarette, gracefully, into an ash-tray, replaced the dark glasses and lay back and looked upwards at the hard and brilliant blue sky. 'Felipe is a contradiction in terms—hard as ice and extraordinarily clear-headed one moment, all fire and malleableness the next. Or at any rate, that is how I see him! I was happily married, but even while I was happily married I was aware of his charm.... I could fall for him very easily, despite what you have just said, if he gave me the least bit of encouragement, and I am absolutely certain that if this strange entanglement with you could be set aside he would give himself up to the sheer, unadulterated joy of loving me! And being loved by me! I have already warned you that he is a man who needs to love, otherwise he will be quite unbearable to live with.... Really unbearable! And therefore it is up to you to grow up before it is too late, tell your grandmother that you decline to be ordered about by her, and—give him up! He will release you without a single qualm if *you* make the effort to win free.... I *know*, that is why I'm glad we've had this little talk, much sooner than I dared to hope we'd find an opportunity to talk——'

Doña Miranda came tapping with her stick along the terrace, in the shade of the overhanging pantiled roofs, and Willow fell silent abruptly, and then warned cautiously:

'Your grandmother is coming! Not another word!'

Angela stood up immediately and offered her chair to her grandmother. Willow continued to lounge in her own chair, and the old woman looked at her with very little in the way of real pleasure in her eyes as she accepted her granddaughter's chair, and relaxed in it with a faint sigh of relief, while her dark eyes remained suspiciously bright.

'Thank you, my child,' she said. 'I find that nowadays walking even with a stick is a great ordeal for me. It is my rheumatism, I'm afraid.'

Then her glance swung coldly round to her future grandson-in-law's favoured guest.

'You are enjoying your stay here, Señora Ruddock, I trust?' she said. 'I saw from my window this morning that you were bathing in the sea. But you are a poor swimmer by comparison with my granddaughter. You may have little on when you enter the water, but the little you have appears to handicap you.'

Willow looked ruefully across at Angela, and smiled even more ruefully. She shrugged her shoulders.... The gesture said plainly that she understood perfectly Doña Miranda did not approve of her, and this was going to be one of her days for making her attitude of mind as clear as crystal.

Angela hardly noticed. She was dwelling upon the conversation she had just had with the widow, and although she was not exactly shaken she had been given a good deal of food for thought.

And when, later, they all drove off in two cars to lunch with a male relative of Don Felipe, who had a summer residence on the same stretch of coast, she was given even more food for thought. Although Felipe saw to it that she occupied the place of honour at his side in his own car, his cold words when they started off had the curious effect of dimming, for the first time in her experience, the golden brilliance of the hot Spanish sunshine.

'I must ask you not to bathe alone in the mornings while we are here, and in fact I would prefer it if you did not bathe at all.'

'But I do not wear a bikini,' she remarked tonelessly, staring through the windscreen at the white road ahead.

'That is not the point!'

'But Mrs. Ruddock wears a bikini, and you bathe with her. Why should not I bathe also, since I do not wear a bikini, and my swimsuit is perfectly respectable?'

'Because it is my wish, and when I make my wishes clear I expect them to be respected,' he replied with a curtness that was like a razor's edge, and left her with little desire to pursue the conversation—or any other line of conversation, if it came to that—with him.

CHAPTER VIII

DON FELIPE'S relative proved to be a very charming elderly man with a weakness for feminine company who was so unlike Don Felipe himself that Angela, at least, was surprised. After more than half an hour of her fiancé's uncompromisingly silent company in the car on the way to the villa she felt the need of a little solicitude and attentiveness, and she got them both from Don José Martinez.

He was quite obviously charmed by her from the moment he welcomed her as she stepped from the car, and although he also paid a good deal of attention to the other ladies it was Angela whose hand he patted almost affectionately as he took it and drew it through his arm as he guided her into the house, and afterwards singled her out as the most honoured guest by placing her at his right hand at the luncheon table.

At the last moment Doña Miranda had changed her mind about accompanying them, fearing the journey would be too much for her in the heat of the day, and it was therefore quite correct that Angela, as a future relative, should receive this special attentiveness. But Angela herself felt quite grateful for it, especially when she noticed once they reached the house that Felipe made a very obvious effort to attract a little limelight to Willow.

She professed to be overawed by the magnificence of the house, with its splendid collection of portraits, valuable china and other *objets d'art*, and Felipe took it upon himself to guide her along the gallery where the strictly family portraits were hung, and pointed out to her various of his forebears who were not represented amongst the portraits in his own villa. And afterwards they disappeared into a little ante-room where cases of medals and priceless manuscripts were on display, and it was quite a time before they reappeared and accepted an aperitif apiece, which the others were already disposing of.

Angela had asked for a fruit drink, but Don José had insisted that she take something a little stronger. He assured her the contents of his wine-cellar were above reproach, and when Felipe reappeared she was standing with a glass of sherry in her hand and looking as if she didn't know what to do with it. Don José lifted his glass high and toasted her with a warm and faintly humorous twinkle in his handsome dark brown eyes, and as Felipe drew near he included him in the toast.

'You have chosen excellently, Felipe,' he told him. 'Your bride is entrancing, and so young I feel outraged by my own advanced years. Were I but a *few* years younger ...' And he smiled and bowed before Angela. 'Need I complete the sentence?' he asked her, with courtly grace.

For the first time since she had become engaged to be married Angela felt that some slight importance did actually attach to her, and even although she was marrying for no really sound reason that she could think of she was glad that, as a result of that marriage, she would acquire one in-law whom she felt absolutely certain she would like.

Felipe made no response to these comments on the quality of his taste, and he seemed quite happy at lunch to devote himself to Willow, who had begun to look a little bored by her host by the time she was escorted into the dining-*sala*. Angela understood perfectly that unless she was offered wholesale admiration she very quickly evinced signs of wishing she was somewhere else. She seemed quite incapable of putting up any form of pretence, even in the interest of good manners.

'I remember your grandmother perfectly,' Don José told Angela at lunch. 'She was a little older than I was at the time of her marriage, but I must confess I admired her enormously ... just as I am now prepared to admire her granddaughter,' and he pared her a deliciously ripe peach and placed it delicately on her plate in front of her, once the dessert course was reached. When it came to coffee Angela found that she was expected to do the honours, her host having no wife or other female relative to perform the service for him, and once again under the watchful eyes of Willow Ruddock she performed the task with the maximum amount of gracefulness and composure.

Willow looked cynically intrigued as the host kissed Angela's small white hand in a most expert and calculatedly charming way as she handed him his coffee cup, but Felipe's expression remained unmoved. He was discussing with Willow the notion of a drive along the coast that evening after dinner, and perhaps a visit to one of the night spots, and apparently her approval of this plan of his was of the very maximum amount of importance to him.

He lowered his voice as he talked with her, and Don José, after studying them for a moment rather closely—and perhaps with a degree of surprise—interrupted by suggesting he should show his fiancée the gardens of the villa.

'It is the hottest hour of the day, but by the sea here there is always a breeze,' he told them. 'And in my gardens you will find a sufficient amount of shade to ensure that our charming Angela is not affected by it. I particularly recommend a visit to the new lily pool I have had constructed. I am rather proud of it, and would like your opinion when you return to the house.'

Felipe was obviously surprised, and equally obviously a little resentful at having any single one of his movements dictated for him. His attitude to his elderly relative was polite and slightly deferential, but unlike most Spaniards of his generation he apparently did not revere old age. He looked as if he was prepared to dispute the wisdom of a visit to the gardens at that hour despite the cooling breezes from the sea, but his uncle made this virtually impossible.

'Come, come, Felipe,' he rallied him with a good deal of dryness—like the dryness of the excellent white wine that had been served with other wines at lunch. 'Must I make myself more obvious and declare that I am still a romantic at heart, and were I your age and engaged to be married I would welcome any opportunity to be alone with my betrothed? You surely understand that I am making a sacrifice by being willing to dispense with the company of your Angela for even a short time?'

At that Felipe stood up, looking a trifle grim, and glanced across the room not at Angela, but at Willow.

'What do you say to examining the lily pool, also, Carmelita?' he enquired of her. 'Or is the exertion too much...?'

But José nipped the idea in the bud immediately.

'No, no,' he exclaimed airily, 'I cannot allow that! I have not so far had an opportunity to talk with Señora Ruddock, and I cannot allow her to go away without repairing such an omission.' He stood up and bowed before her gallantly, the scarlet camellia in his buttonhole threatening to become dislodged from it as he did so. 'Are you interested in ancient coins, *señora*? I have a wonderful collection of which, I think, I am justifiably proud, and I would like to show them to you. I am sure you agree with me that betrothed couples need a little time to themselves, particularly in these so enlightened days ... which are quite unlike the days when I was young. I had to wait until I was married to be alone with my wife!'

Willow cast a horrified glance—an appealing glance, also—in Felipe's direction, but even she realised that she could not be openly rude to her host.... And Felipe had already bowed to the superior will that had ordained he should spend a little time alone with Angela. He took her by the elbow and guided her towards one of the wide open windows, and in a matter of seconds they were outside in the full blaze of the afternoon sun, which came at them with the thrust of a white-hot sword-blade.

'This is ridiculous!' Felipe declared, releasing Angela the moment they were out of sight of the window. 'The old boy must be mad! ... This is the hour for *siesta*, not for the exploration of a garden which seems to me very similar to any other garden along this coast!'

Angela glanced at him under fluttering eyelids. And then the eyelids ceased to flutter and she gazed stonily at her own feet, in their shapely white sandals.

'Of course, if you would rather return to the house,' she said to him quietly, 'I can make my way to the lily pool alone. I do not think your uncle understands the position between us.... He imagines it is not exactly a penance for you to be alone with me, and that is why he contrived this situation. However, I do agree it is very hot!'

He glanced at her uncovered golden head, and frowned furiously.

'You'll get sunstroke, or something of the sort,' he said, seizing her by the arm again and dragging her into the shade of a grove of ilex. 'It isn't as if you are Spanish——'

'Neither is Willow Ruddock,' she remarked. 'And yet you wished her to accompany us!'

He glanced down at her irritably.

'Willow is my guest.'

'And I am the woman you plan to marry? Wouldn't it be nice for you if *I* happened to be simply and solely your guest, and Willow was the woman you were planning to marry?' She turned contemptuous and startlingly clear blue eyes up to him. '*Wouldn't it?*' she insisted.

He still had her by the elbow, and he was thrusting her forward along the path, which led eventually to the lily pool.

'Don't be absurd,' he replied shortly.

'I am not absurd!' Suddenly she came to a halt in her tracks and confronted him. She did something she couldn't remember doing in public before ... partly because her upbringing had forbidden it hitherto, and partly because she had never been quite so angry. And it wasn't ordinary anger—it was helpless, frustrated anger. She stamped her foot on the path, which was evenly gravelled and prevented the sound from carrying very far. 'I hate you!' she declared. 'The very thought of marrying you makes me feel sick! ... And why I didn't run away from school, *and* my grandmother, to avoid this I can't think! It isn't as if I wanted to marry anyone! But to have to marry you! ...'

He looked down at her with his dark face a mask of icy distaste.

'I think you are forgetting yourself, *señorita*,' he observed in a voice that matched his looks. 'Or else you are already being affected by the sun....'

'D-d-damn the sun!' She had never in her life sworn openly before, although her close friend at school in Switzerland had been far less inhibited, and even eloquent on occasion. 'Do you think I don't feel humiliated every time I see you look at Mrs. Ruddock...? And as you obviously find her utterly fascinating *why* didn't you decide to marry her? Was it because you thought she had forgotten all about you, or had married someone else...? Or was it because you do so badly want those estates of mine? You can have them ... I'll give them to you if you'll let me go and tell my grandmother you can't possibly marry me after all! Never mind her indignation. She'll get over it, but I'll never get over it if I have to marry you!'

Her blue eyes were blazing like wild blue stars, and her lower lip was trembling. He looked down at her in astonishment, and the thing that astonished him most about her was the pallor of her face. She was so pale she might have been about to faint, and her whole face was quivering uncontrollably. She put her hands up over her face, and to her own horror she suddenly burst into tears.

'Oh, how frightful,' she sobbed. 'Whatever will your uncle think?'

Felipe caught hold of her by both shoulders and thrust her towards a white-painted garden seat that was placed at precisely the shadiest spot in the long, winding path, and then he made for the lily pool and bent down and soaked his handkerchief in the limpid water, afterwards squeezing it out and carrying it back to her. He sat down beside her on the seat and advised her with a sort of frozen composure:

'Mop your face with this! Stop crying like a baby for nothing whatsoever, and afterwards you can delve inside that handbag of yours'—which, fortunately, she was carrying on her arm—'for any make-up it contains, and do your very best to remove all traces of this outburst in order that we can return to the house. If you return to the house with tears on your face I'll never forgive you.... And I warn you I mean *never*!'

She sobbed hysterically for a moment or so longer, and then she apologised breathlessly, with a painful, sobbing note in her voice.

'I'm so very sorry, Felipe!'

'I should hope you are!'

'I—I don't know quite—what came over me!'

'Don't you?' He sounded very faintly amused.

'No. So far as I—I can remember, I've never made an exhibition of this sort before in public....'

'As there are no onlookers, you can take it I don't consider myself as very highly representative of the general public!'

Suddenly she glanced at him, and just as suddenly she started to giggle hysterically.

'You've got a sense of humour——'

'So, apparently, have you. But don't let it get out of hand. I wouldn't like it to become necessary for me to slap your face.'

Her drowned blue eyes, while she wielded his handkerchief, hung upon his.

'You—wouldn't——?'

'No. It might leave a mark which would attract the attention of my discerning uncle, and as a result draw down upon my head the wrath of your grandmother.'

'Oh, I wouldn't like Grandmother to get to hear of this——'

'Then you'd better work overtime with that powder compact of yours!'

She was working feverishly with a powder-puff, and peering anxiously at herself in the diminutive mirror that was a part of the compact. The delicately tinted powder was achieving miracles, but there were still hectic scarlet patches staining her cheeks, and her eyes were distinctly watery. Whenever she caught her breath it sounded as if she was fighting against a tendency to give vent to another sob or two, and after a silent moment or two of watching her he took the compact from her and slipped it back inside her handbag, placed the handbag between them on the seat, and reached out a long arm and drew her almost roughly up against him.

'You'll do,' he said, 'but you'll have to cut out this habit of being so emotional. Not merely does it destroy your appearance but I personally find it exhausting with the temperature in the region it is at the moment. Besides, it's quite unnecessary. I have asked you to marry me, and it never occurred to me that Mrs. Ruddock would consider taking me on as a husband if I asked her. For one thing, I think she's enjoying her freedom at the moment, and for another those estates of yours really do tempt me. My pride won't allow me to accept them as a gift, so there is no alternative to your becoming my wife.' He swivelled round on the seat so that he could take a good long look at her, and then while she was blushing fierily for no reason that she could actually think of he possessed himself of her chin by squeezing it between his thumb and finger. The pressure hurt a little, but she did not wince. He smiled rather crookedly, lifted his other hand and lightly stroked her cheek, and then said something that caused her to blush more fierily still.

'Do you know, my child, your appearance is decidedly preposessing! You're about as Spanish in your looks as Carmelita, but there is something...' He bent closer and peered at her with greater interest. 'Yes, there is something that is not purely English, either! Although your eyes are so blue they remind me of Doña Miranda, and I'm pretty certain your father didn't have a temper that smoulders like yours ... as if there's a small but active volcano deep down inside you. Are you conscious of the rumblings of a volcano occasionally at the very heart of your being?'

'I—don't think so.' But she smiled as she shook her head.

'You should be. You're highly explosive material!' Then he desisted from stroking her cheek. He sat back and looked at her for a much longer period, and far more thoughtfully. '*Querida,*' he said at last, 'how would you like it if I took you out to dinner to-night?'

'You mean if you took us all out to dinner?'

'Nothing of the sort. My guests can entertain themselves for a single evening, and I'm quite sure your grandmother can be trusted to look after them in my absence. She rather shines as a hostess ... and I hope you will do so, too, one of these days. No, I feel that you and I should make an effort to get to know one another before we are forced into the intimacy of getting to know one another as husband and wife.'

She had possessed herself of the clasp of her handbag, and was maltreating it nervously while she gazed at him as if she was by no means certain that he was serious. Also she looked as if his words —particularly his final words—had covered her in embarrassment. She looked down at the clasp of the handbag, and showed him her luxuriant eyelashes with the bright tips that rendered them extremely attractive.

'What of—what of Mrs. Ruddock?' she demanded in a low voice. 'I mean, won't she perhaps feel that you are neglecting her?'

'Because I transfer some of my attention to my future wife? Don't be absurd, child,' he said.

'But she is rather a—a special guest, and only this morning it struck me that you—do regard her as a very special guest——'

'Which is one reason why you subjected me to that little exhibition just now? No, Angela my dear, you must understand that in many ways I am a law unto myself, and very occasionally even I do not understand why I do certain things. Perhaps I found this visit this morning a little irksome, and was prepared in advance for my uncle's demonstrations of approval where you were concerned. He could hardly show disapproval, since you have everything to commend you in the way of a future wife—looks, youth, family background, by no means a mean dowry. If I had presented Carmelita to him as the woman I proposed to marry he would have looked at me much more askance ... and I very much fear he would have found it extraordinarily difficult to behave with urbanity to Carmelita. Even as my guest he treated her with the greatest caution.'

'Perhaps,' she suggested, without looking at him,

'he is shrewd enough to be just a little suspicious of her.'

'As you are suspicious? And, it is possible, your grandmother is also a little suspicious?'

'I don't think my grandmother exactly approves of Mrs. Ruddock.'

'No, I think she makes that fairly obvious.' Stealing a swift glance at him, she was afraid he was working himself up into one of his own tempers. His dark eyes were beginning to sparkle irately, and the square jut of his chin seemed suddenly very noticeable. She felt her heart sink within her again.

'I don't think it is entirely unnatural that my grandmother should resent Mrs. Ruddock,' she told him very quietly.

She could feel, rather than see, him frown.... And then he stood up, took a few quick strides along the path in the direction of the lily pool, walked back to her and dominated her by addressing her from somewhere far above her head.

'Listen to me, Angela,' he said. 'As yet we are not married, and I still have the right to lead my life more or less as I wish, so long as I remember always that I am committed to marry you. Your grandmother must understand this just as you must understand it. Once you and I are husband and wife I will not, naturally, invite Carmelita to stay unless for some reason you yourself should expressly desire it——'

'That is *quite* unlikely,' she told him distinctly.

He smiled a little grimly.

'How can you really be so certain? You might yet become good friends.'

'Utterly impossible and unlikely.'

'You dislike her so much——?'

'I——'

'Never mind!' He sat down swiftly beside her again and took her hand. 'We will drop the subject of Willow Ruddock for the moment. I believe I asked you whether you would care to dine with me alone to-night, and you have not yet given me any indication that you would. I think it is an excellent plan myself, and I'm sure Doña Miranda will approve. We will take the drive I was planning earlier along the coast, and in a little fishing village where life is very peaceful we will dine. Unless you would prefer some more scintillating spot, with quantities of champagne and very sophisticated company around us.'

'You know very well I would not!'

He regarded her whimsically.

'Now, I cannot really be sure of that, for the last time I took you out to dinner you complained bitterly afterwards because of the lack of champagne and my insistence that you consumed a highly colourful and very decorative ice-cream. I am not sure whether it was the ice-cream or the absence of champagne that really upset you——'

'It was neither.' She peeped at him with a dangerous sparkle underneath her eyelashes. 'It was your attitude ... as if I was a schoolgirl you were taking out to dine, instead of a fiancée. You did not for one moment treat me as if you seriously planned to marry me....'

'If that is really true I apologise very humbly!' But there was an almost gay note of raillery in his voice that didn't quite console her. 'To-night I will treat you as if you were already a matron, and a very mature matron at that. You shall have no cause to complain, I promise you. But now I think we have remained out here in the garden long enough, and if you feel up to facing the combined scrutiny of the others we will return to the house. Let us hope Carmelita has displayed an intelligent interest in my uncle's medals, sufficient at least to maintain him in a good humour. He can be extraordinarily touchy if one rubs him up the wrong way.'

But the host was as urbane as ever when they returned to the house, and only Mrs. Ruddock looked as if she had endured more than enough for one day, and would be thankful when they started for home.

She looked curiously at Angela when she walked back into the *sala* with her fiancé keeping close to her elbow. Angela's face was slightly flushed, and her eyes looked a little over-bright, but that could have been due to the strength and quality of the sunlight. Angela stood looking rather confused in the dimness of the *sala*, which was quite striking after the brilliance of the garden outside, and the host moved forward to enquire of her how much she appreciated the design of his lily-pool.

'You will come again, *cara*?' he said, taking her hand and retaining it between both his soft white plump ones. 'Felipe must bring you often to see me, particularly when you are married.' He looked as if he had said something very meaningful. 'Ah, the marriage! The Great Day! ... How soon shall I be receiving my invitation?' He poked his nephew in the ribs, slyly. 'Ah, you are a lucky one, Felipe ... a clever dog to make certain of such a treasure! She is as pretty as a picture, and I am very nearly in love with her myself. You must let me know what it is you would wish for a wedding present ... give me some idea, at least. And be sure that you consult your future bride on the matter!'

Felipe thanked him punctiliously, and assured him that he would consult Angela. Afterwards he remarked a trifle disparagingly to Angela that he supposed the old boy had something in mind that would tax his bank balance only slightly, for despite enormous wealth he had a reputation which was well deserved for being niggardly.

'Something in the kitchen equipment line would suit him admirably, I'm sure,' he said. 'Preferably one of the humbler items considered important in a kitchen.'

But Angela had taken quite a fancy to Don José, and even if he was mean she was quite sure she was going to like him increasingly as time went on.

'Surely your kitchens are already well equipped,' she replied, with a faint edge to her voice because any mention of her approaching marriage had that effect on her. 'And as you have several houses you must have several kitchens.'

'True.' He glanced at her sideways as they drove back to his villa. 'But there will be only one mistress for all of them ... you! It is for you to decide when something must be added to them! The decision in this case is entirely up to you!'

CHAPTER IX

Hours later he unbent to her in a way he had never unbent before. Having obtained her grandmother's permission to take her out to dine for the second time since their betrothal had been announced, he reacted in a manner that considerably astonished Angela, and might have astonished Mrs. Ruddock had they not been forced to leave her behind at the villa, where she sulkily insisted she was going to be extremely bored for the whole of an unplanned evening.

Angela, wearing her apple green evening gown with the crystal embroidery, wondered as she once more sat beside Felipe in his car as they started off just what he had said to the widow with the smoky-grey eyes and the arrestingly beautiful but sulky mouth that had prevented her from proving slightly awkward about being separated from him for several hours, when he was after all her host. Her friend Johnny would no doubt put himself out to be as entertaining as possible, but Willow had made it abundantly clear, since her arrival at the Martinez villa, that by comparison with Felipe she looked upon Johnny as a poor thing.

Angela felt sorry for Johnny, who was so transparent and so patently adored the lovely widow, following her around like a tame dog when permitted. And when she spurned him and he had to retire discomfited he still only too obviously thought exactly the same of her.

Angela, reflecting upon Willow and her rather too youthful admirer, as the car headed into the last of the sunset, thought how unfair life was when a pleasant and quite inoffensive young man like Johnny could be more or less trampled upon by the woman he adored, and she who was planning to marry a man she did not love was perfectly well aware that, from choice, he would be with Willow at this moment, and no doubt if he was with her he would not be whipping himself up into a state of forced gaiety which had the effect of arousing little response in Angela. In fact, it merely caused her to wonder why he considered the effort it all involved necessary, when the end result would be precisely the same if he sat silent at the wheel and made not the smallest effort to be an entertaining escort.

But after a time she found herself wondering whether he was putting it all on as a kind of act, or whether he was actually looking forward to the evening ahead of them. There was certainly nothing forced about the quality of his conversation, and although it seemed ridiculous he struck her as years younger than when they were being entertained by his uncle, Don José Martinez. And certainly there was nothing repressed about him, as there frequently was when Mrs. Ruddock was a member of the party.

When she asked him where he was taking her, he replied that she must wait and see. Earlier he had talked with enthusiasm of the charms of a small fishing village, and as he had also made a slighting reference to scintillating company she not unnaturally supposed that the place they were making for was not the sort of rendezvous to which he would take Willow Ruddock—despite the fact that he had also promised her champagne and a sophisticated evening.

They drove through several charmingly sited fishing villages, which by this time were all wrapped in the purple bloom that always followed the descent of the sun into the sea, and were twinkling with lights like stars shining through a curtain of gauze. It was the sort of night one could expect on that stretch of coast at that season of the year, and there was in the very atmosphere a feeling of warmth and excitement that rendered the drive a kind of impromptu for the rest of the evening that was to follow. There were heady scents floating in the slumbrous warmth, a sensation like a silken caress as the night wind lifted the hair on Angela's forehead, and as the road climbed they could hear the booming of the rollers far below them, and catch a salty breath of the sea every now and again.

Felipe's car was open, and Angela sat back luxuriously in her seat beside the wheel, thinking occasionally how expertly her companion drove, and admiring the little she could see of his shapely hands on the wheel. Usually he was addicted to speed, but to-night he seemed to have overcome the temptation to cover the ground between him and his ultimate objective in as a short a time as possible, and he even stopped the car on one occasion to point out to her the far-away beam of a lighthouse on a distant point, and the sword-like pathway of light it created on the dark sea.

On another occasion they stopped in order that she could be impressed by a tremendous drop to an unseen beach so far below them that it actually caused Angela to shudder as she peered downwards; and then he indicated a villa on the heights above the drop.

'I used to own that house,' he told her, seizing the opportunity to light a cigarette, although never under any circumstances was he prepared to offer her one. 'It has a magnificent view from almost all its windows, and I liked to come here when I was feeling in need of a kind of spiritual refreshment. Looking at the sea from a great height always has that effect on me.'

She gazed at him in surprise. He had spoken as if he actually did sometimes feel the need of an experience outside anything that could be provided by the life he normally led.

Angela looked up at the starlike lantern suspended above the wrought-iron entrance gate, and she was conscious of regret because he had parted with the house. She, too, enjoyed looking upon the sea from a great height. Even marriage might assume some sort of attraction if part of her married life could be spent in a spot like this.

Felipe glanced at her, with the pale light from the lantern streaming over her fair head and shoulders and etherealising her face. And having glanced at her in his usual casual way, his glance became arrested, as if something had firmly anchored it, and it was several seconds before he looked away. Then he spoke, a little strangely, as he pressed the starter button.

'You have no right to be as attractive as you are, Angela. Some men might have their heads turned completely simply as a result of looking at you.'

Angela answered in some surprise, but in a cool little voice that matched her looks:

'But you don't happen to be one of them?'

'I haven't said so, have I?'

'It has never struck me that you are the sort of man capable of having his head turned by a pretty woman ... not even when she's as outstandingly pretty—or should I say beautiful?—as Mrs. Ruddock. You might admire her, and I'm sure you do, but I doubt whether even she could turn your head.'

'But you do think she has a considerable amount of power over me?'

'Oh yes.... But if I happened to be her I wouldn't bank on it. You are very Spanish, for one thing, and my grandmother has made it clear to me from my cradle that the men of my mother's race very seldom go overboard for their women. It is an attitude of mind, the knowledge they have that

123

women are inferior. Inferior in the sense that they fit into a pattern, I mean, and are, as you might say, always there. Spanish women cannot escape. Of course, I have no doubt at all that they can and do fall in love. My grandmother has tried to make me believe that *when* they succumb to some over-mastering tide of feeling they do so very thoroughly, and that the quality is very different from anything of a similar nature a man of my father's race might have to offer to a woman. But Grandmother is very Spanish . . . I think she's biased.'

'I see,' he said, and his voice sounded very dry as he turned the car away from the sea and they started to climb up into the hills. 'I must say, for a young woman who is contemplating matrimony you have an extraordinarily detached way of look-ing at these things. As the mere man you are about to marry I can't help but feel it is all very unim-portant, anyway.'

'I haven't said so.'

'No, but you certainly indicate as much. You obviously have arrived at very definite conclusions about myself, and apart from that it apparently doesn't trouble you at all that I might be in love with another woman.' He frowned as he drove, his dark eyebrows meeting in a cleft above the faintly arrogant bridge of his nose. 'If that is really true, you certainly astonish me. You quoted your grand-mother just now, but it would certainly surprise me to learn that she married in the state of mind you propose doing. For one thing I can't imagine Doña Miranda submitting to anyone, and for another if she's incapable of jealousy then I'm a poor judge of character.'

She laughed softly.

'Of course she's capable of jealousy. According to her all Spanish women are, and that's what makes life so exciting for them—exciting *enough* for them, shall we say?—when they marry.'

'But you being half English I shall not have to look out for any squalls?'

Once again she answered, 'I didn't say so.' Then her mood changed, and after bending forward to peer with interest through the windscreen at the winding and rather wild strip of road they were covering, she turned her head swiftly over her shoulder and looked at him with a sudden bright and rather provocative smile emphasising the curves of her attractive mouth.

'Do tell me, where are you taking me? This road is not a bit like the coast road, and we seem to be climbing all the time. Is there a village anywhere near? Are we making for one?'

'We are.'

'It seems to me we are travelling a very long way for our dinner. You must know this part of the country well.'

'I do.'

'And when we get there, will it be worth it?'

'It all depends on how prepared you are to enjoy your evening.' His dark, lustrous eyes glanced swiftly at her, and then away. 'If you are prepared to be bored, you will not enjoy it. If, on the other hand, you have not made up your mind in advance that this is to be just another boring and rather pointless evening——'

Her eyes sparkled in surprise.

'I am *never* bored,' she assured him. 'That is, I am not easily bored. Except——'

'Yes?'

'Except when I suspect something has been laid on for me that was the result of boring necessity in the first place.'

He laid a hand lightly over her knee, and patted it.

'Don't worry, Angela! I promised you should not be bored to-night, and I meant it.... And if it gives you any comfort I was not feeling in the least bored when I decided upon the place I would take you for dinner to-night. There might have been one other famous occasion when we dined together and the whole thing fell rather flat, but that is in the past, and it will not be repeated. I give you my word!' he told her again.

Angela surveyed him with narrowed eyes and continued to smile slightly provokingly. She lay back in a more relaxed manner in her corner of the car, looked upwards at the stars that were hanging like bunches of sparkling grapes in the purplish heavens above them, and then once more concentrated on the floodlit road ahead of them. The moon was rising over the whole rather desolate landscape, and it had a magically transforming effect. Angela decided that wherever they were going it could prove unusually exciting.

When they slipped down into a completely deserted village she was disappointed at first. The shadows lay like ebony on the white surface of the road, there appeared to be few if any lights in cottage windows, and they travelled the whole length of the main street before they reached the inn. But once they reached it it was as if a curtain had gone up on a different world. The car-park of the inn was full of cars, and they were gleaming under the silvery rays of the moon. There were so many of them that, once Felipe had helped Angela alight, she was glad to cling to his arm to find a way out of the impasse, and as her small fingers clutched at the immaculate white sleeve of his dinner-jacket he fastened his own fingers over them, and she received an extraordinary sense of comfort and direction, as if everything was perfectly all right, and would have been even had the number of cars doubled themselves.

There was a yellow lantern above the inn door, and an inn sign. Angela could not make out what the sign said, but the warmth of the lantern-light seemed to reach out and engulf her, and it effectively transmuted her pale blonde hair to bright burnished gold, and as for Felipe, his inky dark hair appeared also to acquire a burnished look that was somehow infinitely attractive.

'This way,' he said, and led her up to the inn

door. She could hear music—the throbbing of guitars, and the rippling notes of a piano—even before someone within whipped the door open for them, and the instant he did so the situation became still more transformed. The interior of the inn was quite unlike the exterior, and in fact it was actually an open space with tables dotted around a glistening dance floor, and cascades of flowers drooping above the heads and shoulders of the diners, as well as decorating their tables.

As the result of a swift glance Angela decided that most of the diners were extremely well-dressed men and women, and some of the latter wore the most becoming dresses and a great deal of expensive jewellery. The men had sleek heads and immaculate linen, and in the cleverly diffused lighting their dark eyes sent languishing looks across the tables at their partners, and the partners smiled languishingly back. A few of them were dancing, and in the hot, scented night their movements were leisurely, and it struck Angela that they were like figures in a drop-scene at the theatre.

The throbbing of the guitars, and the rippling notes of the piano, set something moving in the same languid but exciting manner in her own blood, and for a moment she felt startled because the effect on her was so immediate, and she wanted to stand clinging on to Felipe's arm in the entrance, and devote at least a few minutes to feasting her eyes on the scene.

But Felipe led her forward, guiding her amongst

the tables, and finally a waiter brought them to a table that overlooked a glassy strip of water, on which water-lilies floated, and the waiter pulled out a chair for her, and she seated herself and took note of the fact that there were scarlet flowers in a vase immediately confronting her, and the perfume of them was like incense that might very soon find its way up into her brain.

Felipe also seated himself, and smiled at her.

'Well?' he said.

'It's like fairyland. I—I've never seen anything like it before.'

'I don't suppose you have. But there always has to be a first time.' He accepted a menu from the waiter, and consulted it. 'Now,' he told her, 'you must allow me to order for you—as I believe you did once before,' his lustrous eyes suddenly twinkling at her, 'but only because your school had taught you excellent manners, and you believed it was the right thing to do. Now, to-night, it doesn't matter about excellent manners, but it is important that you should enjoy yourself, and therefore I will select all the things you must eat. And of course we must have champagne.... That was part of the bargain, wasn't it?'

He summoned the wine-waiter with a snap of his fingers, and the champagne materialised, and several courses of unfamiliar dishes, so far as Angela was concerned, followed. She discovered that she had an unusually excellent appetite, and afterwards she attributed it to the long and unexpectedly diverting drive to this particular rendezvous, and sampled the dishes without waiting to be invited to do so by her fiancé. He watched her carefully when she took her first few experimental forks-full, and a complacent expression of satisfaction dawned in his eyes when it became obvious that he had chosen wisely. He smiled at her as she looked across at him with a gleam of pure appreciation in her eyes, and as she nodded her head he said:

'It is good, yes?'

'It is very good,' Angela admitted.

The meal was a long-drawn-out, leisurely affair, and while they sat quietly enjoying it at their table the orchestra played and there were several cabaret turns which Angela thoroughly enjoyed. She particularly enjoyed the Flamenco dancers, having seen genuine Flamenco dancers on one or two occasions only, and would rather have enjoyed it—she half suspected—if Don Felipe had followed the example of other male diners and led his dinner partner out on to the glistening dance floor for some active participation during the courses, but being the type of man he was he much preferred to enjoy his dinner undisturbed by exercise, although he was quite prepared to sit back occasionally and judge the floor shows critically from a distance, and even to comment on some of the eccentricities of the dancers.

'Afterwards, if you would care to do so, we will dance,' he said. 'But the food here is far too good to be ruined by jumping up and risking serious damage to one's digestive organs at the same time by gyrating about on that floor there, and in any case my dancing is a little rusty, as you will find out when we do take the floor.'

Angela regarded him across the table as if she was critically appraising him.

'I don't believe your dancing is rusty,' she told him, after dwelling on the matter for several seconds. 'You must sometimes have danced with Mrs. Ruddock, and I'm sure she demands perfection in her partners.'

'Oh, yes?' A gleam entered his eyes, and he helped himself to some sweet water-grapes from the dish of fruit that had been placed on the table. 'You seem to have a very high opinion of Mrs. Ruddock in some ways. She demands, apparently, the best on all possible occasions.'

'Do you think she always gets it?' she demanded of him curiously.

He shrugged his white dinner-jacketed shoulders.

'Who am I to say whether that is possible or not? Whether any one person ever gets the best that is available simply because they desire it, and feel perhaps they have a right to nothing but the best. In the case of Carmelita, she is so extremely decorative that I personally consider the best is just about good enough for her.'

He spoke casually, wiping his fingers delicately on his dinner napkin, but she bit her lip as if he had deliberately gone out of his way to affront her, and she resented it bitterly.

'I do wish you would not call her Carmelita,' she snapped at him.

His eyebrows rose.

'Does it really upset you as much as all that? But we are old friends.... One can call an old friend by a familiar name, surely?'

'She is a *woman* friend. If I had a man friend and I called him by a familiar name, a pet name, you would object, I'm sure!'

'Certainly I would.'

'Well then!' She bit her lip again as he studied her with a look of faint amusement on his face, and that annoyingly complacent air that informed the waiters that he had thoroughly enjoyed his dinner, and a sense of outrage bubbled up in her and declined to be confined within proper bounds. 'I think that is utterly unreasonable!' she told him. 'Our marriage plans go forward, yet you may have women friends, *and* invite them to stay with you, while I—I am to accept it as all perfectly normal, while even my grandmother thinks that it is not normal! And you say you would object if I had a man friend!'

'I would insist that you never saw him again, or at any rate only if you refrained from calling him by his pet name. And even then I should be on the watch for this impostor to make certain he was having the minimum amount of effect on you.'

Petulantly she helped herself to an apricot, and

he reached across and prepared to accept her plate from her in order to pare it in the correct way before she sunk her small and very well-cared-for teeth in it.

'No,' she said, 'I don't think I want it after all——'

'It is a particularly ripe one, and yet not over-ripe. I think you should have it.'

'But I say I don't want it!'

'Do you know what I think is the matter with you, Angela, my child?' he enquired of her in very soft and rather curious tones. His eyes were still partially amused, but there was an unusually soft expression in them as they flickered over her. 'Have you any idea, I wonder?'

Although she hadn't the least idea what was in his mind, she suddenly flushed brilliantly. She lowered her eyes and looked down at the apricot on her plate.

'No,' she answered.

'Would you like me to spell it out for you? Or at least to put it into simple phrases?'

Her eyes remained lowered, and the colour burned so painfully in her cheeks that it actually hurt her.

'I——'

'I think that you are jealous,' he told her, speaking very distinctly. 'I think that you are suffering from your first attack of jealousy—real jealousy.'

Her long eyelashes fluttered, and she looked up swiftly.

'Why, I—wh-what—what do you mean?' she stammered. 'How could I possibly be jealous? What have I to be jealous of——?'

'Carmelita,' he answered, laying down his napkin beside his plate and preparing to rise. 'In other words, Mrs. Ruddock ... Mrs. Willow Ruddock. You are jealous because you think that she and I are on very good terms with one another. Now, shall we dance?'

She was tempted to refuse to budge from the table, but confusion welled over her, and far from laughing or even smiling at her he looked very purposeful and extraordinarily composed, considering the subject under discussion. She had the feeling that if she so much as attempted to create a scene—even though a very minor one— he would know precisely how to deal with her and she would end up in her customary seat in his car with him at the wheel and a long, silent—full of the silence of freezing displeasure—drive ahead of them. And her outburst would have got her exactly nowhere.

So she fought a battle with herself, crushed down the amount of indignation that seethed through her, and stood up and allowed him to take her by her bare forearm and guide her out on to the dance floor.

The band had just begun a tango, and it was one of the old and well-tried ones, full of the voluptuousness of movement and the rhythm that gets into the blood. Despite his admitted rustiness Don

Felipe drew Angela expertly into his arms and swung her out on to the middle of the floor, where for the first time in her life she received a shock of revelation. For far from being rusty he was a most accomplished performer—she had secretly suspected as much—and although she danced well herself she had never before experienced such a desire to acquit herself creditably, and something rather more than that. She was used to dancing with girls for partners, and very young and inexperienced men, so her fiancé's tactics had the effect of depriving her of a measure of her breath when she first found herself circling the floor with him. It was like dancing with something feline and immensely purposeful, and at the same time any deficiencies on her part were easily covered up by his skill. The music, once it had got thoroughly into her blood, set it on fire, and after five minutes she had forgotten everything that tended to underline her self-consciousness and was blissfully aware that this was an experience she might have missed, but which, fortunately, she had not missed.

Felipe's arms held her as if she was a part of him, and she could feel his warm breath stirring her hair. The scent of him, exciting and intensely masculine, seemed to creep up into her brain, and it actually set her senses swimming.

For one second she missed her footing, and he reproved her with a husky laugh close to her ear.

'You dance well, little one, but you hold yourself too stiffly. Let yourself go,' he advised, 'and it will all be so much simpler. Try and forget that we are to be married, and think of me as someone you have met for the first time to-night!'

She had been holding her head stiffly, in the established manner, but she brought round her face swiftly, and found that his was almost alarmingly close to hers. His eyes, bright and mocking with laughter, gazed into hers.

'Would it be amusing, do you think, if we had met for the first time to-night?'

'It might be amusing.'

'But you prefer the knowledge that all the groundwork has been done and in a short time we shall be as close as other married couples? Perhaps closer, since we have still some bridges to cross before we really get to know one another?'

'Do you think we will ever get to know one another?' she returned in a breathless way, her heart hammering against his. '*Really* know one another, I mean, Felipe? It has all been so—formal and arranged! To me you are still a stranger, and I must seem very young and insignificant to you!'

'Not insignificant ... charming.' He looked down into her face with his night-dark eyes, and she was amazed by the luxuriance of his eyelashes at close quarters. 'Exceptionally charming, and exceptionally appealing! Do you know, *querida*, you have the bluest eyes, and the fairest skin! ... I think you are almost unbelievably lovely! One of the first things I shall do when we are married is have you painted!'

'I thought we were supposed to be strangers to-night!'

'Well then, enchanting stranger, I shall endeavour to persuade you—before we part—to agree to have your portrait painted, and then I shall purchase it, and have it hung in my gallery in Madrid where I shall gaze at it often.'

'Won't that be rather expensive, if we are to part again so soon?'

'It is always possible that we will meet again!'

'And if we don't...?'

His arms tightened about her, and for a few seconds she actually found it difficult to breathe.

'You must not say that, *querida*! It would be such a waste! You and I meeting and then going our separate ways.'

'But you are engaged to be married.... Have you forgotten?'

'To you! It was ordained from the beginning of time that you and I would marry!'

'Oh,' she pouted, although her eyes were almost feverishly bright as she peeped up at him through her lashes, 'you are not playing our game——'

The music came to an end, suddenly, and they were left standing like other couples in the middle of the floor and gazing at one another a trifle rue-fully. And then Felipe took hold of his fiancée's arm very firmly and piloted her towards a door that was set in a kind of pergola of roses, and they found themselves in the garden proper of the inn, where the warm, velvety darkness of the night closed in on them on all sides.

'Ah,' Felipe declared, 'it is better here. It was hot in there, and the band is not all that good in any case. Also I find dancing with you a trifle exhausting.'

She tilted back her head and looked up at him. They were standing on a path that she could barely see, and the starshine was creating a silver wonder out of her hair, and the embroidery on her dress sparkled, too. It was so dark that she felt inclined to clutch at him, and he put his arm about her.

'I enjoyed it,' she told him, 'and I didn't find it exhausting. I don't believe you did, either.'

'Perhaps not,' he agreed, a trifle absently. 'Listen!' he said, and she put back her head the better to listen.

The night was filled with the whirring of the wings of countless crickets, and there were birds singing, late though the hour was. The birdsong was piercingly sweet, and it seemed to be wandering on and on like the plaintiveness of a flock of nightingales come to rest in a nearby thicket. Never in her life had Angela been so entranced by birdsong, and she knew that her companion was listening attentively, his dark head slightly cocked, one shapely masculine forefinger still upraised. And then, with his arm still about her, he drew her along the path.

'The night of the singing birds,' he murmured softly, as if to himself. 'We come all this way to be entertained by a natural choir that is many times more delightful than that brassy din in there,' jerking his head over his shoulder towards the lighted inn. 'Do you not agree, little one?' drawing her fingers through his arm and holding them there as if he had arrived at the firm intention never to release them.

Angela was silent, and he paused and put his free hand under her chin and lifted her face, tilting it so that the starlight fell full upon it.

'You don't agree, is that it? You prefer man-made noises?'

'I enjoyed dancing with you,' she repeated. 'I—I —I don't think it ever occurred to me that you were such a wonderful dancer!'

'I can hold my own with most men of my years.'

'And many younger men. I don't think I saw many men in there dancing as you can dance.'

'You should not have had eyes for other men! You should have been savouring to the full the delight of getting away with me, hanging upon my every word and seeing nothing but me! As it is you seem to have been taking in quite a lot apart from the excellence of my performance on the dance floor.'

She shook her head at him, smiling.

'No, Felipe, I am not interested in other men.'

There was rather a long moment of silence, and then he tilted back her face so that he could look right down into her eyes, and he saw his own image reflected in them, between him and the brightness of the stars.

'That is ... true, *querida*?' he asked her very quietly.

'Perfectly true.'

'Sometimes I think you are very young and that all this is not fair to you. It was never a secret dream of yours to marry an Englishman?'

'Not really.'

'You have no lingering regrets? You would not rather I talked to your grandmother and persuaded her that these are modern times and a modern young woman has a right to make up her own mind about the man who is to be her partner for life? For you know there will never be any question of divorce between us! Once married to me it will be for life ... perhaps beyond life, if the union is very close.'

She felt as if wild thrills were coursing up and down her spine, and even her finger-tips tingled as the same wild thrills travelled along every important nerve artery in her being. Her soft lips parted, and she found it difficult to breathe ... as if she had been running up several flights of stairs and had not paused on the way.

'That is how I would like it to be, Felipe,' she told him, and for the first time she knew that she had uttered words to him that were no more, and no less, than the truth. In a sense she astounded herself, having persuaded herself for weeks that she was not interested in him as a man, and that all she was doing in going forward with this marriage was adhering to her grandmother's wishes. But now, all at once, they were both aware that the situation was changed in some very subtle way.

Felipe murmured something in Spanish that she did not quite catch, and then his white teeth gleamed as he smiled at her in the starlight, gripped the firmness of her little chin more closely for a moment, and then released it and encircled her with both his arms. He drew her up against him, held her against a heart that struck her as working overtime, unless it was purely her imagination ... muttered something huskily in Spanish, and then addressed her very clearly in English.

'Your grandmother would not approve of this, but this is not a moment when your grandmother's wishes should remain paramount. I have the highest possible regard for her, but we have a duty to one another, and there is something I must find out. Look upon it in the nature of an experiment if you wish, but do not afterwards report on it one way or the other to your grandmother....'

And before she properly realised what he intended, his mouth had found and taken possession of hers, and the sensation that she had been running up and down stairs increased tenfold as the first truly adult and important kiss of her life had the effect of altering the whole of the rest of her life for her, and from the moment he set her free she knew that she would die—possibly just wither away and die—if he never kissed her again.

She stood holding trembling fingers over her lips

while he stood looking down at her with wise and tender and utterly transformed dark eyes, and then he said gently that they had better return to their table and settle their bill, and then he would drive her home.

'And I think you can forget to-night, my darling. ... But not, of course, if you don't want to! And where Doña Miranda is concerned, not a word! Come now,' placing his hand lightly on her shoulder, 'let us leave the birds and this garden and go inside and settle our debts.'

As they walked back to the inn she said quietly, not looking up at him but staring straight ahead:

'At least to-night has taught me one thing, and I am indebted to it for that. I must often have behaved in a very foolish fashion in the past!'

CHAPTER X

THEY drove back to the villa in a silence that could have been described as companionable, although underlying the silence there were still many leading questions that went unanswered. Angela no longer felt frustrated, and she had a sufficient amount to think about to prevent her wondering very seriously whether the preoccupation of her escort was entirely normal after the recent revelation in a deserted inn garden; and also she was very sleepy, and she actually dozed once or twice during the homeward journey, receiving a gentle pat on the knee and a murmured word from Felipe each time she woke up.

When she finally woke up after a really prolonged nap the journey was over, and they were back at the villa. The house was in darkness save for the lantern over the front entrance, and Angela gathered that Mrs. Ruddock and her three friends had either already gone to bed or were not yet home. From the silence of the house, and the fact that the lights were switched off in the hall, she suspected that they had gone to bed.

No doubt Willow Ruddock had been profoundly bored, and boredom had driven her to seek an early night.

Angela realised that her grandmother had been in bed probably for hours, and she had no intention of disturbing her.

Apart from a slight flick of her cheek and a, 'Sleep well, little one!' from Felipe, she received no further indication that he regarded the evening as a pronounced success, and a great step forward in the path of their future life together. In fact, she was disappointed when he made no attempt to kiss even her hand, and the sense of disappointment accompanied her up the dark polished staircase to her room, where it crept with her into bed and prevented her sleeping as dreamlessly as she might otherwise have done.

In the morning she woke early—before the sun was up, in fact—and breakfasted alone in her room, afterwards going along to her grandmother's room to give her an account of her outing on the previous evening. Doña Miranda lay watching her very shrewdly as Angela described the drive along the coast, the inn where they had had dinner, and the singing birds in the starlit garden. The sound of the garden and the singing of the birds seemed particularly to interest Doña Miranda, but she did not make any actual enquiries as her granddaughter sat swinging her legs on the side of her bed, and looking down demurely at her linked hands.

From the girl's expression there was nothing to be learned that could have been described as of any real interest, at any rate to a close relative who had the girl's interests very much at heart. But the slight guardedness of her expression did somewhat intrigue the old lady.

'And so you enjoyed yourself, child?' she enquired at last.

'Oh yes, Grandmamma.'

'And you certainly looked very delightful when you set off with Felipe. I was quite proud of my only grandchild. Did Felipe admire the green dress?'

'I think so.'

'He didn't say so?'

'He said I looked ... Yes, he did say I looked very charming.'

'I should think so!' The words sounded like a snort, and it was very seldom that Doña Miranda descended to anything so unladylike. 'If he did not think you looked charming he would have been as good as blind!'

Angela didn't see anything of the others that morning, although she gathered they were on the beach. Felipe appeared at lunch, but he appeared very abstracted, and it transpired he had been doing some business in the local town that morning. He was very much afraid he might have to leave them and pay a visit to Madrid before the week was out, and that immediately set Willow Ruddock pouting, and drew from her quite an angry protest.

'Oh *no*, Felipe! You abandoned me last night, and I was very, very bored—so bored that I went to bed at a ridiculous hour. You can't go all the way to Madrid and leave us to entertain ourselves.

After all, we are your guests,' she reminded him, draining the dregs of her final cup of coffee and setting the cup down delicately in its saucer.

Felipe looked along the length of the table at each of his guests in turn. His glance seemed to linger longest on the young couple who had accepted his invitation for a week, but now seemed disposed to linger on indefinitely.

'If there is anyone who would care for a trip to Madrid I shall be pleased to have their company when I leave tomorrow,' he told them as if he suspected that one or two of them, at least, might jump at it. But the young couple, who were thoroughly enjoying their extended holiday, and had no very real reason why they should rush back to England now that their hotel bills were being taken care of, remained silent. Only Willow spoke up eagerly.

'Take me with you, Felipe.'

He glanced at her, and it seemed to Angela, who was sipping the remains of her own coffee, that his glance lingered on her speculatively. And then he said:

'No.... No, I think not. It is better that you should remain here.'

'But it will be so dull without you!' She ignored the fact that it was Angela who should have made that remark. 'And if there's one thing I simply can't endure for long its dullness! Besides, if you take me with you I won't trouble you at all, I promise you! You can drop me off at a hotel. I can look at the shops and get my hair done by someone who really knows something about hair, and then when you are ready to return you can pick me up again and we will return together. How is that?'

His dark, thoughtful eyes continued to dwell on her.

'I shall be staying at my club,' he warned her. 'I shall have much to do, and there is no question of my being in a position to show you anything of Madrid. Not that, as I am aware, you need to be shown Madrid.... You know it already. But you could be as dull in your hotel as you will be here.'

'Impossible,' she declared, hypnotising him—or obviously trying to—with her huge, smoky-grey eyes. 'There isn't a soul in the world who could be dull in Madrid. It's the most exciting capital I know. *Please*, Felipe,' she pleaded, and quite obviously the concentrated attack from her grey eyes won. He capitulated with a slight air of irritability, and folded his napkin with impatience.

'Oh, very well,' he agreed, and rose to leave the room. 'But I warn you once again it is a business trip I am making, and you will not see much of me in Madrid.'

Willow mocked him contentedly.

'Who said I wanted to see anything of you in Madrid?' she retaliated, with a bright sparkle in her eyes, and a gay, upward curve to the corners of her unbelievably lovely mouth.

Angela left the dining-room in the wake of her fiancé, and caught up with him in the middle of the cool, echoing, flower-filled hall. He halted and glanced over his shoulder at her with obvious, although very slight, impatience, as she called to him breathlessly:

'Felipe! May I have a word with you before you go to your study?'

'Of course, *cara*. But I have a number of letters to write, and very little time to spare.'

Angela braced herself.

'Won't you take me with you to—to Madrid, Felipe? I, too, could do some shopping, and——'

He gazed at her with over-simulated horror.

'And your grandmother? What would she have to say?'

'She would understand. I—I could make her understand.... And why is there so much difference between taking me and taking Mrs. Ruddock?'

'Mrs. Ruddock is not my fiancée.'

'No, but doesn't that make it rather—rather worse....'

She was horrified because his expression all at once grew extremely cold. And the sound of his voice froze her a little.

'I'm not at all sure that I approve of an implication of that sort, Angela,' he told her, as if instead of being engaged to be married they were strangers who disliked one another. 'There is a certain amount of vulgarity about it, for one thing, which I deplore. I'm quite sure Doña Miranda would deplore it even more. Now, if you have nothing more urgent to communicate to me, allow me to get on with my letters. It is important that I do not miss the afternoon collection of mail.'

'Oh, very well, Felipe.'

She drew back, and he went on his way to his study, closing the door after him once he had disappeared inside it with a snap. She bit her lip. So the situation wasn't really altered ... although after their evening outing together she had been prepared to believe that it was.

Doña Miranda had had lunch in her room on a tray, so she had not heard the conversation that had resulted in Felipe agreeing to take Willow with him to Madrid. But when, the following day, the two of them set off in Felipe's car she expressed the view that Felipe had acted very wisely. He would almost certainly leave the widow behind him in Madrid when he returned—or he would if he had any regard at all for the strictness of Spanish conventions, and the nearness of his approaching wedding. Doña Miranda confessed that she had not been at all happy at the continued presence of Mrs. Ruddock in the house, but she was prepared to acknowledge that it was difficult to get rid of an invited guest, who was also a friend of some standing, if the friend was unwilling to leave. She rather suspected that Felipe had acted in a highly diplomatic manner.

But the girl who had acted the part of maid to Mrs. Ruddock admitted, when pressed by Angela, that there were still a large number of her things left behind her in her room. If Felipe intended to get rid of Willow he was planning to do so without the least suspicion on her part. And of course it would be a simple matter to send her things on after her.

But somehow Angela was not as confident as her grandmother. In fact she was not confident at all.

She was swimming in the sea a few days later when Felipe returned. The first she knew of his return was the sight of his car—very familiar by this time—approaching the villa along the coast road, and she extended her bathe far beyond the normal length of time she devoted to this daily exercise because of some new shyness which prevented her from hastily seizing her towel and drying herself and slipping back into her clothes. Another reason was a dislike of appearing before him dishevelled, before she had had a chance to do anything about her face and her hair; and yet another was distinctly more primitive.... She was afraid. Afraid to find out whether or not Mrs. Ruddock had returned with him.

The sun was slipping low into the sea and the beach was growing dusky and the outlines of the rocks uncertain when she finally got together all the shreds of her courage and made for the house. It was brightly lighted by this time, and there seemed to be a good many voices all talking at once, and a good many pairs of feet racing up and down the stairs and along the corridors as she slipped in by means of a little-used side door.

Felipe was in the hall, talking faster and more furiously than anyone else, and when he saw her he advanced towards her and grabbed her by the shoulders and dragged her under the full blaze of one of the lights.

She thought that his face looked thin and pale, and his features were set.

'*Where* have you been?' he demanded. 'Everyone in the house has been searching for you, and your grandmother is upstairs having hysterics because no one had the least idea where you were, and apparently you've been missing for hours. What in the world have you been doing? And why did you slip off and do it without informing anyone where you were going?'

'I've been bathing,' she answered, moistening her lips with her tongue because her mouth felt dry, and tasting sea-water as a result. 'There was no reason why I should tell anyone that I was going for a bathe.'

'No *reason*?' She was quite certain he was going to shake her, and she actually tensed herself to resist him as his fingers grasped her shoulder more brutally. But evidently his better instincts got the better of him, for he refrained. 'How often have I told you that this is a dangerous coast, with strong undercurrents, and that you must never take any risks? No wonder your grandmother is upset! I've been back here for over an hour and at least you might have been on hand to greet me! Instead of which I have to submit to having the whole house thrown into a kind of turmoil.'

She managed to shake off his hand, and despite the fact that her hair was still a trifle damp, and her whole appearance was generally rather bedraggled, she managed to draw herself up to her full height and look as if she really was a very dignified young woman who couldn't understand why such a fuss had been made because of her absence.

And the one thing she did not believe was that her grandmother had been having hysterics.

'I think you are making a great deal out of nothing at all,' she told him in a clear voice that was very faintly edged with a strong note of scepticism, since in her opinion he really was making an extraordinary fuss, and she couldn't think why. 'Sometimes I bathe for only a short while, and on other occasions I like to remain down on the beach for as long as I feel I am unlikely to be missed. When I went down to the beach you had not returned.... How was I to know you had returned from Madrid?'

The coldness of his face began to alarm her. He turned his back on her, walked away across the hall and then flung round and walked back to her.

'How were you to know?' he echoed her, a biting note of sarcasm in his voice while his dark eyes flashed. 'As my future wife you might have spent a little while each day anticipating my return—or so I would have thought! And as this is the most likely time of the day to expect my return you could have been actually looking out for me, rather than going through the motions of a mermaid down there on the beach.'

'I see.' Suddenly she thought she realised why he was angry.... He was annoyed because she had not been looking out for him. And then down the handsome main staircase came a graceful figure, beautifully made-up and perfumed and ready for the evening ahead of her, and wearing a dress Angela had certainly never seen her wear before, and which she therefore deduced was new—almost certainly bought in Madrid—and which made her look quite exquisite.

It was black ... perfectly cut, obviously extremely expensive black. And with it the radiant widow, whose hair had also been set in an entirely new style, wore a single white gardenia, tucked in at the low bosom of the gown.

She stood at the foot of the staircase, giving a pat to her hair as if to make certain not one single strand of it was out of place, and then lifted her eyebrows as her smoky-grey eyes alighted on Angela.

'Oh, so there you are, my dear!' she exclaimed. 'The whole house has been in an uproar because there seemed to be some sort of idea that you were missing. Why, I can't imagine.... Unless Felipe suspects you of making assignations that do not include him!' She advanced towards the figure of her host's fiancée, smiling between the fringes of her outrageously long and luxuriant eyelashes, giving off a wave of French perfume with every mood. 'I say, my dear, you do look a mess!' she told her placidly. 'As if you've been fished out of the sea! Did someone try and drown you while we were away?'

Angela made a darting move forward to the foot of the staircase, and at the same time Felipe called her name sharply.

'Angela!'

But she disappeared up the stairs, fled along the corridor which led to her own room, and fastened the door securely once she was inside it. From the room on the other side of the bathroom which she shared with her grandmother, she heard Doña Miranda's voice calling in an unruffled manner:

'Is that you, child?'

'Yes, *Abuela*.' Breathless after her wild flight up the stairs, she pushed open her grandmother's door and saw the old lady sitting complacently in a chair near the window. If she had suffered any great alarm recently there was nothing in her appearance to indicate that she had.

'Felipe, I understand, has returned,' she observed. 'And I gather that Mrs. Ruddock has returned with him.'

'Yes.' Angela stood chewing her lip in the doorway.

'I suspect that something went wrong with Felipe's plans, and that is why he has brought her back with him.' Such infinite faith in Felipe shook Angela slightly, as well as aroused a good deal of

154

astonishment because Doña Miranda was apparently extraordinarily simple and trusting, and declined absolutely to think the worst of her future grandson-in-law. 'We shall have to put up with her presence here a little longer.'

Angela enquired rather bluntly:

'Have you been anxious about me, *Abuela*?'

'Not excessively so, child. I thought you remained rather long down there on the beach ... but I could see you from my window, and I was not anxious. What makes you think I should have been?'

'You were not in an hysterical condition a short while ago?'

'Most certainly not!'

Angela withdrew into the bathroom. Before she closed the door she said quickly, reassuringly, to her grandmother:

'It's all right, Grandmamma. It was just that I heard you were worried, and I had to find out. I'm so sorry if you thought I stayed too long on the beach.'

'But I didn't, I assure you, child——'

Angela closed the door of her own room before the sentence was finished, and she drew a long breath. So Felipe had invented her grandmother's hysteria, and his anger had been caused by something else. Very likely he wanted to impress upon her his right to restrict her movements, and it would have flattered his vanity much more if she had waited on the doorstep for his return. The fact that she had been calmly enjoying herself in the sea had annoyed him ... and the fact that he had thought it necessary to humiliate her in front of servants and guests—and in particular one guest, Willow Ruddock!—had had a most peculiar and decisive effect on her. For the first time she formed the resolution to be independent ... really independent! He had no rights over her yet ... and as a result of his trip to Madrid and his return in a very black humour accompanied by his lady friend who had been doing some extremely expensive shopping in Madrid, and had the air of one who had made up her mind about the charms of that particular corner of the coast, she was far from being absolutely certain that he ever would possess those rights over her.

She was in fact still trembling with indignation and the reaction after being so painfully humiliated, and she made up her mind she would not join them for dinner that night, and if Felipe didn't like it he could make clear his objections when he saw her again the following day. And by that time she might be more ready to answer them.

Whether or not Felipe was in any way discomposed by her absence at dinner she had no clue to his reactions that night. She went to bed declining to partake of anything on the tray that was brought to her by one of the maids, and the house struck her as very silent and still, although she did hear music later on in the evening. She lay listening to it, soft piano music, and she guessed it was Willow amusing herself at the piano in the *sala*. And later still someone took to strumming a guitar, and she guessed it was one of the other guests.

She slipped out of bed and looked out of the window at the dark line of sea, with a late-rising moon just beginning to cast a silver light over it. She thought she saw figures moving down on the shelving white sand, and two of them were keeping close together. With a slightly sick feeling of revulsion inside her she asked herself whether those two figures were the figures of Felipe and Mrs. Ruddock ... with that exciting French perfume clinging to her as she moved down on the sands, in the gentle, caressing warmth of the night.

In the morning she got up early and bathed by herself in a sparkling blue sea. At that hour she usually felt at her best, but after a sleepless night and a multitude of unresolved doubts gnawing at her she was conscious of an unusual lassitude, and she merely floated on the water, remaining hidden in a trough of creamy waves as the others made their way down from the house for a first dip of the day.

She dived and floated just above a garden of coral and weed as they took to the water. She could hear the voices of the young married couple, and she had already glimpsed Johnny Hainsforth, with Willow and her host the last to make their way down from the house. Willow this morning was wearing a floral bikini, and her bright hair was loose and flowing round her shoulders, for she always disdained to conceal it beneath a cap—just as Angela herself disdained to wear a cap.

She could hear Felipe's voice, sounding just a little impatient and edgy as Willow called something to him, a trifle mockingly. There was a clear laugh from Willow, and then a challenging cry as she struck out for the breakwater, and a violent churning up of the water as Felipe plunged in and followed.

The others were merely amusing themselves in the water, but Willow was in a perverse mood, and she was determined to prove to Felipe her prowess as a swimmer. Actually, she was far from being a strong swimmer, and usually she admitted as much to herself and everyone else and contented herself with floating gracefully on her back and looking like a mermaid in the water. But this morning, for some reason such tricks did not appeal to her—or not any longer—and she called out triumphantly in the sun-warmed air that she was challenging Felipe to a race.

Angela was crouching in the shallows as the floral bikini shot past her, but somewhat to her surprise Felipe did not follow in pursuit. He shot off at an entirely different angle, and whether she knew it or not Willow went on her way without any attractive male host cleaving the water in her wake and ensuring that, should she get into difficulties, he would be on hand to go to her assistance.

It seemed rather strange to Angela, but she assumed that the two had had some sort of a tiff, and Willow was demonstrating her femininity by provoking him with it and no doubt anticipating the result with some excitement. Angela had never been able to decide whether she was physically attracted to Felipe, or whether it was his wealth that attracted her, but she did know all at once that the widow was recklessly courting danger, for apparently she had no knowledge that the bay was full of cross-currents, and she was heading straight out into the middle of it in the confident anticipation of being followed.

Angela was not a particularly strong swimmer, but she had collected quite a few medals for her aquatic performances in the past. She had even won a medal for life-saving. And now she received the peculiarly strong impression that her skill in the water might be tested in a very short while, and if anyone was to benefit from that impression she ought to keep Willow Ruddock in sight at least. So she struck off after her, swimming cleanly and silently, and managed to keep the bright gold head ahead of her in sight without giving any indication that she was following in pursuit. In order to do this she swam partly under water all the time, and when Willow looked back challengingly over her shoulder there was no sign of her. There was no sign of Felipe, either, and this annoyed the widow so much that she struck out even more recklessly. She was quite sure Felipe was somewhere on hand, but he was remaining hidden beneath the waves in order to give her a fright—or teach her a lesson, perhaps.

She decided to give him a lesson. She was revelling in a sense of freedom and rebellion one moment, and the next she was overtaken by cramp, and the resulting horror threw her into absolute panic. Instead of resting herself and giving the attacked limbs a chance she turned for home and the nearest beach, and started to thresh out wildly like an utterly inexperienced bather. She even called out, in terror, and Angela, who was not many yards away, suddenly surfaced and swam to her rescue.

Willow caught sight of her and was filled with wild relief.

'I'm drowning!' she called. 'I've got cramp!'

'Keep absolutely still,' Angela cautioned her, 'and let me grab hold of you! Whatever you do, don't struggle!'

But Willow was in such a state of panic that struggling was inevitable, and so soon as Angela was alongside her she grabbed at her, and it took all Angela's skill to maintain them both afloat. Willow's hampering grip was not merely choking her it was preventing her from sticking to the rules of live-saving and getting them both back to shore, and the knowledge that unless she could control the widow's panic and get the better of it they were both in danger of ending their existence in the sparkling blue sea, under that unclouded sky, caused Angela, for the first time in her life, to feel the rising tide of panic herself.

Gasping, she managed to call instructions.

'You'll have to let me go! You *must* let me go or I can't——'

Willow was blue in the face, and her eyes were staring. She clung like a limpet around Angela's neck.

'Save me, save me!' she moaned. 'If I let you go I'll drown, and you'll be pleased.... Felipe will be pleased! Oh, why doesn't someone save us both ...?'

A masculine voice in Angela's ear stilled the panic that was getting out of hand.

'All right, I've got her! You can let go, and try and unfasten her hands from your neck.... Willow,' he ordered, 'let go of Angela and I'll get you back to shore. You're quite safe now! There's absolutely nothing to be afraid of! Just relax completely and leave everything to me!'

His voice—and almost certainly his strong, sustaining hold—acted like a charm, and Willow responded immediately and instinctively, letting go of Angela and sinking back into his arms. By this time she looked as if she was on the edge of unconsciousness, and he concentrated on manoeuvring her into a position that would enable him to swim with her to shore, and while these manoeuvres were taking place Angela was of necessity forgotten. In any case, he probably had little fear that, relieved of her burden, she couldn't fend for herself, and she kept out of reach until he was heading strongly and surely for the distant yellow line of beach, and then, with her neck smarting from the indentations Willow's nails had made in her flesh, she struck out after him and followed in his wake until he was treading water and carrying Willow up the beach. There the others were all grouped and waiting for them, and as Johnny Hainsforth was the most anxious amongst them there was no lack of assistance in restoring the inert widow to full life and vigour again. She had swallowed a lot of water, and it took some time before she was able to sit up and recognise them. Then she moaned continually, and insisted that she had had a terrible time and it was nothing short of a miracle that she had been saved at all. She seemed to think that Angela, instead of helping her, had been willing to leave her to drown, and her condemnation of his fiancée at length drew a short, sharp reproof from Felipe.

'But for Angela you almost certainly would have drowned,' he told her. 'I couldn't possibly have got to you until it was too late, and in any case Angela was doing her very best for her. I think she's got a few scars on her neck that will prove that to anyone with doubts.'

He looked round for Angela, but she had grabbed her towel and her beach-robe from behind the rock where she had left them, and made a quick disappearance up the beach to the house. He directed at the shimmering sea behind him a searching glance to make certain she was not still at the mercy of the waves, and then concentrated his attention once more on Mrs. Ruddock.

She was looking more like herself now, but she was still very pale, and her eyes were unnatural hollows in her pinched cheeks. He crouched down on his knees beside her and demanded to know why she had been so foolish.

'I thought you were following me,' she explained.

Felipe shrugged his shoulders. There were occasions when women were a little too much for him, but at the same time he was obviously greatly concerned for this one. He insisted on carrying her into the house, had the local doctor summoned, and supported the latter with emphasis when he prescribed rest and warmth.

'You must rest in your room, at least for several hours, Carmelita,' he told her. 'Everything is all right now, but you have had a shock. It will take some little time to get over it.'

The doctor agreed with him. The *señora* must rest, and advised her host to take the maximum amount of care of her. He was a small, dark, susceptible man, and Willow in one of her most attractive house-gowns, with a certain amount of colour returned to her cheeks and her eyes very darkly grey and appealing, lying on a couch before an electric fire, was well-nigh irresistible... or so he would have asserted had he been asked for his own very private opinion.

He had not so far seen Angela, and it occurred to him that Felipe was making such a fuss over the lovely English lady that he probably had plans for marrying her. And the doctor couldn't find it in his heart to blame him. It was one thing to admire one's own countrywomen, but when one came across such a specimen as Mrs. Ruddock one either succumbed outright or was very difficult to please indeed.

The doctor departed, promising to look in on the following day, and Willow settled down on her couch before the electric fire, which had successfully abated her shivering attacks, and prepared to make the most of being a temporary invalid. As a result of what had happened to her that morning Felipe, who had been a little casual sometimes during their stay in Madrid, was being most attentive. Indeed, she could hardly wish for him to be more attentive.

When Angela saw her fiancé again he was dressed and looking rather grave and controlled. She had dealt with the livid marks on her neck with a lotion which had taken a lot of the sting out of them, and covered them up further after the application with a dusting with talcum powder. But nevertheless they still showed, and she had been keeping out of the way of her grandmother in case the old lady, who had very little time for Mrs. Ruddock, should have something to say about the method by which she had acquired them. In Angela's present state of mind it was no time for any awkwardness involving Willow Ruddock.

'I sent a message up to your room to enquire

whether you were all right,' Felipe told her, his eyes on the marks which were not entirely hidden. 'The maid said you were resting.'

'Yes, I—I did feel a bit all-in after what happened this morning,' Angela admitted, by no means anxious to make the most of her own feelings, but hardly yet recovered from the shock of his complete lack of interest in what ultimately happened to her after he himself had rescued Willow.

He went across to her and, taking her by the shoulders, moved her into the light. He frowned as his eyes studied her neck.

'These should have been looked at by the doctor while he was here,' he observed.

She shrugged off his hands with impatience.

'What nonsense! They are only scratches! Besides...'

'Yes?'

'There was enough furore in the house without my adding to it when the doctor was here. With Mrs. Ruddock to attend to I don't think he would have thanked you if you had presented him with another victim.'

Felipe continued to frown. Despite the fact that she backed away from him all the time he managed to catch hold of her again and cupped her face with one of his hands. He looked down at it, taking note of its paleness and the dark circles under her eyes. There was no doubt about it, there was strain in her eyes, too, and their blueness seemed to have a dark, opaque quality. They also held a kind of open distaste that was new to him.

'What is wrong, *querida*?' he asked her gently. 'I thought you were in control of the situation this morning, apart from those evidences of the struggle you had with Willow, and it never occurred to me that I should have made more effort to get you to shore, too. You are such an excellent swimmer, and I know you've acquired a lot of trophies. I thought you would have resented it if I'd made a fuss over the occurrence; and besides——'

'You had Mrs. Ruddock to look after. I know!' Her lips tightened so much that they appeared thin and contemptuous. 'Naturally, you must have been dreadfully upset because she had such a narrow escape from drowning, and one could hardly expect you to have eyes or ears for anything else while your anxiety lasted—certainly not a fiancée who was all part of a bargain! I'm sorry, Felipe, but when you failed to remember my existence this morning I realised that I couldn't possibly marry you. You'll just have to accept it that I *can't* marry you, and perhaps something can be done about those estates of mine! Can't I make them over to you...? A Deed of Gift, or something of the sort? I assure you my grandmother will be the first to recognise that my failure to keep to our bargain justifies your insistence that some recompense shall be made to you! Oh, I know you haven't insisted yet ... but naturally you will!'

Felipe's hands dropped away from her as if he

had been stung. He regarded her at first with astonishment, and then his dark eyes narrowed and his whole face grew hard as a rock.

'So, *señorita*,' he said softly—the words so soft that they alarmed her slightly—'you think I will insist on the fulfilment of our bargain, do you?'

'Yes.' She stood before him, almost defiantly, and no one would have guessed that she was enduring a kind of agony deep down inside her. 'A bargain is a bargain, after all, and we Cazenta d'Ialgos——'

'Oh! So you are a Cazenta d'Ialgo now, are you? I thought you were very proud of being a Grevil!'

'I am.' She drew herself up to her slim height, and the blue eyes were undoubtedly very proud indeed. 'But the Grevil half of me is English, and English people do not enter into the kind of agreement you and I entered into—or into which other people entered on my behalf. As a Cazenta d'Ialgo I am committed to become your wife, because my grandmother decreed that it should be so. Also as a Cazenta d'Ialgo I have to sumbit to my grandmother. But as a Grevil I have the right to change my mind, provided my withdrawal from our contract does not involve you in any material loss, and that is why I suggest that a Deed of Gift be drawn up making over to you the estates you covet.'

Felipe stood staring at her for a moment longer, and then he started pacing up and down the room, his head bent.

All at once he came to a halt again in the middle

of a valuable Persian rug, studied the pattern of it as if he had never noticed it before, and had never before been struck by its intricacy, and then put back his sleek dark head with the movement of an arrogant horse who suspected a hidden fence and was firmly determined not to cross it in any event.

'So, my dear,' he said, 'you wish to retract your word, do you? Erase your signature, in fact, for I believe we signed a document committing us to marry. There were various provisions in it that your grandmother insisted upon in your interests, and as you say there were provisions that concerned myself, and which would make me the loser if some unfortunate happening prevented our marriage. Well, I might as well tell you here and now that I have no intention at this late stage of being cheated ... and that means I don't mean to be cheated out of you, quite apart from the estates on which you set so much store. I have a mind to make you my wife, and I shall make you my wife!'

'No.' She was alarmed because he looked so cool and determined, and her agony was increased because he was so cold-blooded about his intentions. While she wished the floor would open and swallow her up and thus prevent her from having to face a future without him, he was almost brutally informing her that, whatever her wishes, he was not prepared to yield an inch when it came to a question of his rights.

She straightened her shoulders. She felt like

someone whose secret aspirations were being dragged in the mud, but her determination not to marry him never wavered for an instant. Not after his complete disregard of her that morning, and his obvious preference for Willow Ruddock.

She tried tempting him, even taunting him.

'If you do not marry me you will be able to marry Mrs. Ruddock! With a part of my fortune and all your own vast possessions that is a prospect that should look very tempting to you.'

He shook his head, smiling at her in a way she did not in the least like.

'No, my dear, I have no intention of marrying Mrs. Ruddock.'

'Then you can make her your mistress, and you will still be able to lavish my money upon her!'

His whole expression altered. The expression in his dark eyes frightened her, and she had never seen quite such a coldly curling upper lip.

'If you were of the opposite sex I would thrash you for that!' he told her curtly.

Then he once more turned away, walked over to the window and looked at the sea—that had provided him with quite a tussle that morning—spoke to her without turning his head, and with the greatest incisiveness.

'It is a pity you appear to have become obsessed with the subject of Mrs. Ruddock. I have suspected for some time that you rather enjoyed looking upon her as a kind of rival. However, whether or not she is your rival I have no intention of setting you free, and whether or not I would sooner marry Carmelita I intend to marry you! It may be a sacrifice on my part, but I choose to have it that way. Whatever you say to your grandmother I shall unsay, and the wedding arrangements will go on as planned. In point of fact, the date is now set for three weeks from to-day—in Madrid. You and your grandmother will be returning to your own house and make your final preparations, and two days before the wedding you will be accommodated at a hotel in Madrid. It is all arranged. There is nothing ... nothing that you can say that will alter it!'

She had turned very pale—even paler than when she entered the room. She swallowed twice, and licked dry lips.

'That is absurd, Felipe,' she told him coldly. 'You know you cannot possibly command my obedience. I am a human being.... Not a horse you are thinking of adding to your stables.'

'A horse or a woman.... It is all the same! You will be mine soon!'

He turned triumphantly, and his bleak eyes travelled over her. She felt as she had felt in the beginning of their acquaintanceship—as if a closer tie with him would be something like a nightmare. And knowing now how utterly ruthless he was, and could be whenever it suited him, she was suddenly frankly appalled.

'I will leave you to dwell upon our conversation,'

he remarked, making for the door. 'It is high time I made some enquiries concerning the well-being of Carmelita. The doctor insisted that she is in a very fragile condition!'

CHAPTER XI

ANGELA waited in the room until his footsteps had died away in the corridor outside it, and then she tore open the door and rushed upstairs to her own room. Her cheeks were burning with a mixture of humiliation and pent-up emotion. The last thing she wanted to do was run into her grandmother just then, and so she secured her door by locking it, and she also took the precaution of locking the door which communicated with the bathroom, and beyond it Doña Miranda's room.

It was still early in the day, and Doña Miranda had gone for a walk in the gardens. Angela at last became convinced of this when she heard no sound on the other side of the bathroom door.

What was she to do? She lay on her bed and thought of all sorts of desperate and retaliatory measures that she might take, including enlisting her grandmother's support because Felipe was so obviously enamoured of Mrs. Ruddock, and if only Doña Miranda could be sure of it she might call a halt to the wedding herself. Angela thought she could convince her if only she talked long and earnestly enough to her—and also if she drew her grandmother's attention to the scratches on her neck.

But instead of doing that she finally rose and bathed her face with cool water, powdered her nose and touched her mouth with lipstick and her eyes with a little mascara, covered up the marks on her neck with a fine chiffon scarf, and went downstairs when the luncheon gong sounded to join the rest of them at lunch. The rest of them, that is, with the exception of Mrs. Ruddock. For once Doña Miranda joined them, and she expressed genuine concern over the near disaster that had overtaken Felipe's most charming English guest early that morning. For some reason Angela's part in the rescue—or, at any rate, not a very active part—was not made clear to her.

No one would have guessed, looking at Felipe while the long-drawn-out meal lasted, that he and his fiancée had been discussing separation only a bare hour or so earlier. He looked as if every emotion of which he was capable was completely under control, with the exception of the concern he felt for Mrs. Ruddock's well-being, and even that could have been nothing more than the natural concern of a host judging by the almost complete absence of expression in his eyes.

That afternoon, while the rest of them took their customary siestas in their rooms, and in the coolest corners of the garden and the shore, Felipe departed in his car to execute some business he had mentioned casually at lunch. Angela once more lay on her bed and wrestled with her problem without getting appreciably nearer to solving it, and her grandmother in the room next door, knowing nothing whatsoever about her problem—so far as Angela was aware—dozed placidly in her comfortable long rattan chair beside a window that had its shutters securely fastened over it, and the whole house, standing as it did beside the shimmering sea, was as silent as a pool.

The afternoon hours dragged away, and at five o'clock one of the maids brought Angela a tray of afternoon tea. In the room next door her grandmother also sipped tea with lemon, and found it very refreshing.

There was the problem of the evening. Angela did not feel she could go downstairs and take part in conversation with the others—their numbers probably reinforced by Carmelita, whom the maid who brought the tea had informed Angela was very much recovered, in fact almost completely recovered, and preoccupied with selecting a dress for the evening.

No, Angela thought, making up her mind firmly and unshakably for the first time in her life, she would not go downstairs and join the others, and if possible she would not be drawn into conversation with her grandmother, who tried once or twice to gain admittance from the room next door.

'Please go away, *Abuela*,' she pleaded through the door. 'I have a headache.'

'I have some excellent Cologne that should help you, child,' her grandmother called softly through the door.

But Angela declined to open the door. Whether or not she convinced her grandmother that her headache was too painful to enable her to talk to anyone for any length of time she did not know, for Doña Miranda went away, and from the silence inside her room she went downstairs to dinner that night, which Angela had in her room on a tray.

No one else enquired after her. There was no message on the tray ... not even a command from Felipe. And she was left to make the most of her self-imposed seclusion knowing, or at any rate believing, that no one really cared—not even her devoted grandmother—and to all intents and purposes the rest of her future life lay in ruins about her.

But this was an attitude of mind which lasted until she had drained the last of the coffee in her coffee-pot, and then abruptly—as if someone had swept cobwebs away that had been clouding her mind and her thinking powers—she arrived at a decision. By the time Doña Miranda came upstairs, tap-tapping along the corridor with her stick, her granddaughter was waiting for her.

'Grandmother!' She burst into her room through the dividing bathroom with an immensely purposeful look on her face—such a look Doña Miranda had certainly never seen there before. The old lady was looking rather pale and tired, as if some unusual exertion had taxed her considerably, and as she stood leaning on her stick and regarding her granddaughter there was an extremely patient expression on her face, as if she was keeping her natural impatience in check, and was prepared to be reasonable.

'Well, child?' she demanded. 'I trust you enjoyed your dinner in the seclusion of your room? At your age I was not permitted to take a meal in my room ... not unless I was ill.'

'When you were my age, *Abuela*, things were different,' Angela told her. 'They were very different! Young people had to obey their parents, and they were not allowed to think things out for themselves ... not in Spain, anyway. But even in Spain to-day things are not the same. The young do have minds of their own, and if a course of action is objectionable to them they have a right to protest. I have decided that there is one thing I cannot do, and therefore I've got to tell you so, and it doesn't matter what you say, *Abuela*, I won't change my mind....'

'*Well?*' Doña Miranda demanded, as if her patience was rapidly evaporating, 'what is it? Don't make speeches, child. Just get to the point!'

'I can't marry Don Felipe!'

'I thought it was that. And if it is nothing more than that I agree with you that your wishes in this matter have never been properly taken into account. It was *my* wish that you should marry Don Felipe, and I still believe he is the right man for you, but after much dwelling upon the matter in the last few days I have, like you, arrived at a conclusion. No one must force you to marry Felipe,

176

and if you honestly are very strongly against marrying him you must give him back your ring!'

Angela literally gaped at her.

'But, Grandmother....'

The old lady looked as if this was almost, but not quite, the last straw.

'It seems you are difficult to please,' she remarked a trifle acidly. 'But I will tell you this.... If you hadn't come to me with the truth as you have now done I was going to insist that you opened that door between us and listened to what I have to propose. I don't want any histrionics or any well-thought-out diatribes. It is perfectly simple, you being absolutely clear in your mind about the amount of esteem in which you hold Felipe. You must go away at once, and leave me to make your peace with Felipe! To become involved with him in argument would be fatal—although I understand you have been a little forthright to him earlier in the day. That is not the way, however, to handle Felipe! You can take a horse to the water, but you can't make him drink!'

Angela was twirling her engagement ring on her finger.

'Do you mean to tell me, Grandmamma, that you have discussed me with Felipe...?' she asked as if she was faintly perturbed by the very idea.

'I wouldn't say we discussed you,' her grandmother returned, limping to a chair and sitting down on it. 'But I did have something to say about Mrs. Ruddock's continued presence in this house, and as my granddaughter I felt that—well, you had certain rights!'

'And Felipe?' Angela enquired still more thinly.

'He didn't exactly agree with me, but I suspect that the charms of this alliance that has been arranged between you are beginning to pall a little. When the marriage was contracted you were reasonably amenable, but recently it has been obvious to anyone with eyes to see that you were growing rebellious. A marriage in which the wife rebels from the outset would hardly commend itself to a man of wide interests who likes peace and harmony in his background. A wife to come home to.... A wife to welcome him is one thing, but a wife who would behave like a fishwife every time she lost her temper or considered herself ill-used is quite another!'

Angela's pale face coloured indignantly.

'I did not behave like a fishwive, *Abuela*, and I never have behaved like a fishwife,' she protested. 'If Don Felipe prefers to rescue another woman from the sea and leave me to drown——'

'Which you did not do,' her grandmother pointed out to her.

'No, but I might have done.'

'However, you are safe and sound, and with all your swimming trophies and your undoubted prowess in the sea I consider that Felipe would have been very stupid indeed if he had considered for one moment that you could drown in a perfectly calm sea just because of a slight tussle in the

178

water with a silly Englishwoman who has no prowess at all. Don't you realise, child, that anything might have happened to her in her wild, hysterical state if he hadn't been very firm with her, and given her all his attention?'

'I still say he might at least have looked around to make sure I was all right,' Angela muttered sulkily.

Doña Miranda surveyed her with an absolutely blank face, and the same air of increasing weariness.

'But, apart from this deplorable neglect on his part, you are not in the least in love with Felipe, is that it?' she asked.

'I—er——'

'*Are you?*' the older woman shot at her.

'No,' Angela answered, and wondered whether she had ever told such a deliberate lie in her life, and to her only living relative, too. Something of the confusion and the bitterness in her heart showed in her face; the natural recoil on her part from committing herself to a blatant untruth; and if there was one thing Doña Miranda had it was a pair of sharp eyes.

However, she persisted with her probing.

'You have no softness for him whatsoever? If he married this—this Englishwoman it would not upset you?'

Angela hesitated, went very pale, and then answered with a blatant 'No.'

'Then, in that case, the way is clear.' She pressed

a bell for the maid, and while they were waiting for the girl to answer it explained the plan she had formed. 'You will leave here to-night. I have already arranged with Felipe's chauffeur to drive you back to Granada, and all you need take with you is one single suitcase of your clothes. The rest will be packed tomorrow and will accompany me when I return. Naturally, there are many things to be worked out with Felipe, but I don't think there will be any acrimony on his part, and I certainly shall be as diplomatic as I know how. When I return to Granada we will discuss your future, and perhaps it might be a good idea if you are sent away for a while——'

'In disgrace?' Angela blurted out, as if this was in the nature of a final straw.

'No, not precisely in disgrace.' But the words her grandmother left unsaid spoke volumes. 'However, we cannot expect that a broken engagement will escape being commented on by all our acquaintances, and there will be many unpleasant duties I shall have to perform before the thing can be decently overlooked and, we hope, forgotten. You have a wedding dress awaiting you in Granada, and presents are arriving there every day.... That ring you are wearing will have to be returned!'

Automatically Angela removed it from her finger.

'And Felipe?' she enquired, in a strange, husky voice. 'You must have discussed something of this with him already if he is willing to allow his chauffeur to drive me back to Granada. You say I am to leave to-night. Is he downstairs, and am I likely to see something of him before I leave?'

'Fortunately, there is no danger of anything of that sort,' Doña Miranda replied, with the first note of complacence she had allowed to enter her voice. 'You couldn't possibly wish to see him before you leave, and I happen to know that he has taken his guests for a drive along the coast, using one of his other cars. They are unlikely to return until it is very late, so you can make your escape without running into any sort of unpleasantness before you do so.'

Angela bit her lip, and her little teeth pressed so hard into her lower lip that it bled.

'It sounds to me as if all this has been arranged with the connivance of Don Felipe,' she remarked, not entirely surprised because of the complete absence of sympathy in her grandmother's face, but bewildered nevertheless because of this sudden opening of the doorway to freedom. And as for Felipe.... Well, it might well be that he would gain something from this financially, but she never would have believed—especially after their quarrel that morning—that he would let her go quite so easily.

If nothing worse, it was humiliating ... it was the most humiliating thing that could ever possibly happen to her, which probably indicated that she was by no means balanced in her reasoning.

Her grandmother looked at her with sudden,

real impatience.

'What do you wish, child?' she enquired of her acidly. 'To eat your cake and then complain that there was neither cream or jam on it?'

'It isn't a matter of cream or jam.' Angela continued to bite her lip, to tear at it agitatedly. 'But——' And then she turned away to her wardrobe. 'Do you think Felipe will marry Mrs. Ruddock, *Abuela*?' she enquired hurriedly and breathlessly as the maid's footsteps sounded in the corridor.

Doña Miranda answered as if the question actively offended her, and was the final proof of the general bad taste and decadence of modern young people like her granddaughter.

'How should I know, child?' she returned with even greater acidity. 'Do you think that I sat downstairs after dinner discussing with Felipe his relationship with a woman of whom I most certainly do not approve, and actually asked him whether he proposed to marry her? Do you imagine I have no pride, and no sense of the fitness of things? I may be afflicted with a granddaughter who has neither, but at least I have sufficient for both of us!'

Angela went on her way to the wardrobe, but just before the maid entered the room she had one final question to ask.

'So you did discuss all this with Felipe after dinner?'

'We had a short talk in his study. His guests were

waiting for him, and it had necessarily to be brief.'

'*Well!...*' Angela thought, and snatched open the door of the wardrobe and began dragging her clothes out willy-nilly.

CHAPTER XII

The maid went ahead of her with her suitcase when she crossed the hall. The house was uncannily silent, and there was only a very dim light left burning in the hall, with its polished furniture and handsome Martinez portraits lining the walls. Angela glanced up at one or two of them before she reached the door and the short flight of steps which led down to the drive.

What was it Felipe had said?—Not once, but twice! 'The first thing I will do when we are married is have your portrait painted, and you shall hang in my gallery in Madrid!'

She felt an appalling—almost a shattering—sensation of loss, not because her portrait would never hang in his gallery in Madrid, but because she herself had only too plainly been put right outside his thoughts already, and while a lonely journey to Granada awaited her he was driving his friends along the coast!

Her eyes became so blinded by the rush of self-pitying moisture that filled them that she scarcely saw the steps once she had set her foot on them, and it was the maid who prevented her from falling as she returned to the house after handing over her case to the chauffeur, who had already deposited it in the boot of the car.

'Be careful, *senorita*!' the maid cautioned, and as she uttered the caution the chauffeur turned from closing the boot and took a half step towards the front door as if he, too, was anxious to prevent an accident.

It was extraordinarily dark outside on the drive, and Angela realised it was because the powerful lights above the entrance door, and on each side of the entrance gate, had not been switched on.

But the car lights were streaming like sword blades down the drive, and the car itself was headed for the main gates.

The maid said a polite farewell to the departing guest, whom she had understood was proposing to marry the master in a matter of a few weeks or less, and Angela found herself placed in the back of the car, with a light rug over her knees because a cool wind was blowing in from the sea and lowering the temperature dramatically.

They cleared the main gates and started to hum along the main coast road, but Angela was hardly aware of anything about her, and the only thing she sensed was the alarming extent of her own black depression. It was of her own free will that she was returning to Granada freed of the shackles of an engagement about which she had protested constantly in the past, and she knew that only a few weeks ago—less than a few weeks!—she would have been conscious of an overwhelming sensation of relief because at last her grandmother had seen sense and made it possible for her grand-daughter to live a life of her own selection.

But unfortunately for Angela there had been a visit to a remote inn and a night in a garden full of the sounds of singing birds that had made it as clear as a searchlight to her that she didn't want to live a life of her own selection. And even before that her ideas had been changing, the personality of Don Felipe Martinez had been exercising a kind of fatal charm. And now that she knew just how fatal that charm was she had severed all links with him, and only that morning she had hurled at him all sorts of accusations that she now bitterly regretted.

But it was too late—too late!—to do anything about it. She and Felipe had parted, very likely for ever, and the fact that she had fallen desperately in love with him was the final bitter pill that she had to swallow.

'You are comfortable in the back there, *señorita*?' a quiet voice enquired from behind the wheel.

Angela almost froze in her seat. There was something about that voice, despite its lowered tones, that was as familiar as her own right hand.

'If you would prefer that I close one of the windows I will do so,' the chauffeur offered amiably, drawing in towards the side of the long and empty coast road. 'There is quite a noticeable breeze from the sea to-night, and we cannot have you catching cold.'

The car came to rest beneath an umbrella pine, with a breathtaking view of a moonlit sea on their left hand, and not a soul in sight anywhere on their other hand, behind or ahead of them. Angela made a sound in her throat which sounded as if her utterance was being slightly strangled, and then following another, greater, effort she said quite clearly:

'Felipe!'

'Would you like me to close a window?'

He had alighted and was peering in through her rear window at her. Then he opened the door and tossed his chauffeur's cap on to the back seat of the car with her.

'Of course it is I, Felipe! Whom else did you expect would be driving you back to Granada?'

She put a hand up to her mouth and was silent for a moment. Then she gave an uncontrollable sob of relief.

'Oh, Felipe, I am *so* happy!'

He indicated by means of holding the rear door wide that he expected her to alight and join him in the front of the car. And as she fell in with this new arrangement with the maximum amount of hurry she found that his arms seized her as her feet touched the grassy verge, and she was crushed up against him and his mouth was pressed against hers almost brutally; but as soon as they were both in a position to speak he reviled her in no uncertain terms for making it necessary for him to stoop to this piece of deception, and putting her grandmother to a good deal of unnecessary strain in the process.

'I really ought to put you across my knee and slap you,' he told her, kissing her feverishly at the same time to prove that he had no intention of doing anything of the kind. 'You have harped upon the subject of Willow Ruddock for so long and so persistently that to-day I honestly felt I couldn't endure any more! Just because she was my guest and I had to look after her.... Just because she would *insist* on returning with me from Madrid, and I had to appeal to your grandmother to help me to get rid of her!'

'And what was Grandmother's suggestion?' she asked, as she leaned against him languidly in the full splendour of the moonlight, and felt so full of gratitude and thankfulness that she knew she could never express the extent of it.

'To do nothing,' he replied, 'except put forward the date of our wedding. And as a matter of fact, that was one thing I did in Madrid, and if it's any comfort to you I never *saw* anything of Willow once I got her to Madrid, and I certainly wouldn't have brought her back here with me if I could have talked her out of it. But she had left all her things behind, and she put forward the excuse that she wanted to pack them herself. And there was Johnny Hainsforth.... She wanted to collect him.'

'Was it because you were not on very good terms that she took such a risk in the sea yesterday morning?'

'I imagine so. I am not a vain man, but it was difficult to dislodge her.... Why, I cannot tell you, because she is an extremely rich widow. If, as you imagined, it was my possessions that attracted her, they did not.'

'She is in love with you, of course,' Angela told him, clinging to his arm passionately and looking up at him adoringly. 'Who, in their right senses, would not be in love with you?'

'I can think of one young woman who wasn't only a very few weeks ago,' Felipe replied with a certain dryness.

She shook her head at him in wonder, her silky golden head which he was stroking.

'I must have been mad,' she declared. 'Or else I was just obstinate! You see, I'm sufficiently English to want to make my own decisions, and my grandmother treated me constantly as if I was wholly Spanish. It was simply a question, I suppose, of asserting myself. But now I know that I couldn't... - Oh, Felipe, I couldn't live without you!'

He answered in a somewhat uncertain voice:

'You don't have to, *querida*.'

'And you're not in the *least* in love with Mrs Rudd——?'

'If you say that again,' he warned her, in a far from uncertain voice, 'I really will do something violent to you that I shall afterwards regret!'

'Such as?' she tempted him, her eyes like stars as they hung upon his.

'Until we are married there is nothing very

much I can do to you except kiss you,' he replied in a frustrated manner. 'But *once* we are married, I warn you, my provoking little one, that unless you submit to me absolutely I will be quite ruthless with you!'

'I will submit to you absolutely, Felipe,' she promised him, and even as she did so she wondered what had happened to all her English independence.

They stood there for several minutes longer at the side of the deserted road and the sea, under the umbrella pine, and then she stirred in his arms and finally disengaged herself.

'And what now?' she asked. 'Where are we going now?'

'To Granada,' he replied. 'I am taking you, as arranged, to your grandmother's house, and then I shall return and pick up your grandmother, and after that we will all proceed to Madrid—and after that we will be married!'

Suddenly Angela heard herself laughing a little hysterically. For the first time it had struck her as funny—really funny—that her dignified grandmother should have lent herself to this masquerade.

'I always thought I knew her—really knew her,' she told Felipe, as he opened the car door for her, and she got in beside the driver's seat. 'I imagined she would never do anything that was not absolutely correct. But to allow us to travel like this to Granada together, with not a *duenna* in sight, is not correct, is it?'

'If you are Spanish it is not perhaps correct, but if you are English ... why, certainly.' And Felipe showed her his white teeth gleaming in his dark face as he smiled at her sideways. 'But do not forget, my darling, that in a very brief while you will be wholly Spanish, and then, most certainly, it will be a different matter! Everything you do from now on will be very Spanish!'

Angela lay back against the luxurious car upholstery, and she sighed with delight because in future she would not be in a position to exercise her independence. And she marvelled that she had ever imagined it was the one thing she wanted to do.

Have You Missed Any of These
Harlequin Romances?